Medusa's Proxy

A PARANORMAL MONSTER ROMANCE

CORALIE MOSS

Published internationally by Pink Moon Books, British Columbia, Canada.

ISBN: 978-1-989446-31-7

❀ Created with Vellum

Acknowledgments

Massive thanks go to my writing crew at WORDMAKERS; to author K. Sterling for the initial impetus; to author Katrina Carruth, who beta-read this story over the 2021 holidays; and to my husband, who encouraged me to let my freak flag fly.

About the Author

Author Coralie Moss likes to start her Fantasy stories with witches and other Magicals and plunk a surprise or five into their seemingly normal lives. This bi-coastal, dual-citizen divides her time between Massachusetts and Salt Spring Island, British Columbia—the site of much magical inspiration—with her husband and two rescue cats.

Join Coralie's mailing list for book news, giveaways, short stories, and the occasional homage to apples.

Also by Coralie Moss

The completed Shifters in the Underlands series includes:

- **Paper Dragon** (book 1)
- **Blood Dragon** (book 2)
- **Moon Dragon** (book 3)

The completed Sister Witches Urban Fantasy includes:

- **Once Blessed, Thrice Cursed** is book #1 of the Sister Witches Urban Fantasy Series. Set in Northampton, Massachusetts, it introduces us to Clementine, Beryl, and Alderose Brodeur.
- **Demon Lines** (book 2) is the continuation of Clementine's story.
- **The Scarab Eater's Daughter** (book 3) gives us the sisters' continuing adventures from Alderose's point of view.
- **Beguiled, Bewitched, & Broken** (book 4) features the middle sister, Beryl.
- **The Sister Witches Urban Fantasy Series: Box Set 1** (includes book 1-4)
- **Witches Everbound** (book 5) completes the Sister Witches Urban Fantasy series.

The completed Calliope Jones series of novels includes:

- **Magic Remembered** (book 1)
- **Magic Reclaimed** (book 2)
- **Magic Redeemed** (book 3)
- **Magic Restrained, a novelette** (book 3.5)
- **The Magic Series Box Set #1**

· · ∗ · ☾ · ∗ · ·

Join Coralie's mailing list for news & ongoing short stories.

Contents

Prologue: Medusa's Gift

It can be terribly hard to recover from a beheading.

Impossible, some would say, to live again once your head has been separated from its rightful place. But moments after the blood spray resulting from Perseus' fatal stroke birthed an army of venomous serpents and a winged horse sprang from the stump of my neck—surprise, didn't see that one coming!—my sisters took possession of my body and secreted it off to a sacred shrine.

Assured by the priestess in charge she had the magic and the means to keep my organs viable, Sthenno and Euryale left me in her care. The two Gorgons then shadowed my beheader, caught up to him undetected, and switched my distinctive head for one cobbled together from an earlier chop-and-drop and a handful of snakes who owed me and my sisters a debt.

We'd saved the serpents' scaly hides from becoming potion ingredients; they could act like deadly little monsters and save me from becoming a footnote in history. Medusa, yet another mortal woman victimized by a goddess who chose to take out her frustrations on an innocent, rather than face the root cause of her discontent.

Did I carry "baggage"? Of course, I carried baggage. Poseidon violated me. Athena punished me, not him. And Perseus... Well, thanks to Zeus's sword and my sisters' swift actions, Perseus did me a favor.

Hundreds of lifetimes and a handful of body modification practices later, I'd created a version of me that others could live with. I'd filed my fangs into a demurely sexy look. Altering my golden hands required finding a tattoo artist who worked with metallic inks. A banished demon hiding out in Prague covered my skin from my wrists to above my elbows with lacy filigree. The effect was so stunning, House Chaumet used me as a hand model for their iconic bracelets and rings for most of the nineteenth century.

As for my "terrifying visage," AKA the snakes that replaced my waist-length blond locks, I covered my head, face, and shoulders with enchanted veils. I could see out, no one could see in, and not a single inadvertent death stained my path.

Those centuries of loneliness and longing took a toll on my psyche, however, and I was ready to toss my raggedy bags over a bridge, come out of hiding, and engage with the world. To do so, I had to first do something about mes petits serpents, because as long as I wore the seven asps atop my head, I would never be able to have a long-term relationship with anyone, be they lover or friend.

I'd had both mortal and immortal beings take an interest in me, and I'd always, always made it clear to each that me and the covering I wore to hide the snakes were inseparable. To those who shared my bed, the novelty of a masked lover inspired sensual reverence right up until the moment they uttered some variation of "Just once, Medusa. Please?"

Their plea became a death knell to whatever bond we'd built. I would say no, and my lover and I would shoulder on until one of us left, after which I would invariably swear off all but the most casual of intimate relationships. Exhausted by the constant cycle of letting go, and the absolute predictability of human nature, I started to see a therapist. She spoke about the power of fear regarding intimacy and trust and suggested I work on releasing my "issues" before seeking another lover.

The therapist was very popular, probably because her advice worked for humans. I thanked her for her insight, gave myself a pep talk, and signed up for a lengthy desert meditation retreat. I knew my sisters' quick actions had given me a second chance at life.

Now I needed a first chance at love.

Determined to find a way to safely drop my veil and show my face, I walked desert trails day after day, considering my options in silence and gradually strengthening my resolve to find a way out of my predicament.

I received a summons from my friend, Habonde, on the penultimate day of the retreat.

To the modern world, the Goddess of Plenty was worth a few scant paragraphs in an online encyclopedia. Few knew that whenever a glass of ale was lifted, or a celebratory fire lit, it was her they honored. I'd gravitated toward Habonde the moment we were introduced. Months later, she invited me to join the Alliance of the Forgotten and Disremembered, a loosely config-ured group comprised of faded stars from myths and legends.

In Habonde's note, she said she admired my fortitude in the face of my ongoing "shitty situation" and asked if I would come *to Scotland for a few days of pampering and to discuss an idea. She gave no details, other than this idea involved relieving me of my most burdensome problem for a set period. She also reminded me to please wear my veil or dark glasses so as not to inadvertently turn her or any of her staff to stone.*

I appreciated her candor, along with the offer to stay at her rustic-yet-luxurious retreat in the Northern highlands. When I arrived, two of her acolytes escorted me to a room where slippers and a plush robe awaited. They also presented me with a box of locally sourced live mice for my famished little darlings, enabling me to leave the girls in their carrier and submit my travel-weary body to a massage and a seaweed wrap.

That night, after a splendid dinner, Habonde started off our dessert and digestif with the question: "When was the last time you had a day off?"

"A day off from what?" I responded, cutting into the generous slab of baklava oozing with honey and chopped walnuts with the edge of my fork.

"A day off from being you, Medusa. A day off from hiding who you are, what you are, out of fear you'll turn someone to stone, thereby alerting all of Mount Olympus to the fact you're alive."

"Oh, they know I'm alive," I assured her once I'd licked my deliciously sticky lips. "They choose to ignore me." Honestly, I was fine with being disregarded and though Habonde's hearth enveloped me in its warmth I shuddered at the thought of re-engaging with Olympus' ego-driven, consequence-shunning crowd. I hurriedly shoved another bite of baklava into my mouth.

"What about your sisters?" my hostess probed, reaching

across the table to shake out my napkin and dip a corner in the finger bowl.

"Steenie the Mighty and Eury the Far-Roaming? What about them?"

"I wager they could use a day off too. Wouldn't you three enjoy spending more time together?" Habonde waved the napkin at me. "You're welcome to use this place any time."

I set my fork on my dessert plate, dipped my fingers in the flower water, and reluctantly cleaned my face. I'd become so used to living and traveling alone, I'd gotten out of the habit of reuniting with my sisters over rituals and festivals and the like. I hadn't thought to ask them to join the Alliance and guilt stabbed my gut. "I can't remember the last time the three of us got together and did much more than drink to our sorry fates in the darkest corner of a pub."

"Then it's settled." Habonde leaned back in her padded chair. "Medusa, I want you to take a year off."

I raised my snifter of Bénédictine and sipped at the herbal liqueur. "A year off from what? I have no job I yearn to be free of, no passel of children nipping at my heels."

"Are you willing to be one of my beta-testers?"

"Tell me more." Ah, now we were getting to the meat of the evening. A servant appeared with the bottle of liqueur. My hostess waited to respond until our glasses were refreshed.

"You, Medusa, shall be the first member of the Alliance to have a fully-trained proxy."

"A proxy, as in a stand-in? A substitute?"

"Exactly. Some years ago, I awoke from the first of many dreams urging me toward a project. I resisted at first. After thousands of years living and practicing in obscurity, I'd grown... comfortable, complacent even. Until the final dream."

She suddenly took to her feet and raised her arms, looking upward as though her vision hovered between us and the ceiling beams. "I saw my shrines reborn as places of study and training. The world and its inhabitants need magic now more than ever, and I knew I was to become a teacher."

Habonde bent to retrieve the napkin that had slid down her skirt to the floor while she spoke and settled into her chair. "I sent out feelers via social media sites like Faebook, Flutter, and InstaScram. I posted the world over, reaching out to young Magicals who felt they had lost their way, or never found their way in the first place, never had proper training from their family, their schools, tribes, covens.

"I vetted the first wave of applicants personally, then sent them to my primary shrine here in Scotland. Once they committed to the program, my acolytes set to training them in the ways of tending to mythologicals like us.

"After completing their training, the plan is for them to apprentice with other forgotten Beings in need of daily atten-tion, affection, and adoration. Through that attention, our sistren in myth and magic will regain enough of their stature to re-enter the world and resume their rightful place, or at least receive a nice nudge in that direction. The apprentices will gain useful life skills and precious insights into living with magic."

Golden rays of long-dead sensations pulsed behind my ribs. Was that optimism? *Could that be* hope? *I knew it wasn't the brandy. Gripping the carved lion heads on the ends of my chair's arms, I leaned forward. "I want to be your* alpha-tester. *Do you have someone in mind for me?"*

Habonde pressed her lips together in a self-satisfied smile. "I do. I plucked her from the hills of a small town in New Hamp-shire—that's a state on the North American continent. Her mother is fae, her father is human, and our girl's led a reckless life."

I hmm'd. This girl's story wasn't all that unusual for the magically blessed. "Either she rejected her magic, didn't have enough magic to make much of a difference, or she had no idea she had magic in the first place."

"Bingo on the second option. Her magic is latent, but it's there. She's got artistic talent and what she really wants is to study sculpture. First, though, she needs discipline. She needs to learn to care for something other than following her latest whim only to drop it in a week or bedding her latest crush and running the moment emotions enter the picture. Hers or theirs."

The warmth from those golden rays dimmed a little. "Gee, Habs, you make her sound so... desirable."

"Oh, she is, Medusa. She is." Habonde practically glowed as she held my gaze through my darkened lenses. "She just needs to build faith in herself and tap into her potential. And you and your story and your seven-pack of serpents are her ticket to autonomy."

Reassured, I relaxed my grip and cradled my snifter. "And what name does this diamond in the rough go by?"

"Madeline Mallow Meadows LaFleur. She likes to be called Maddie."

·· · ☽ · ·· ··

Medusa's Proxy

Chapter One

MADDIE MEADOWS

"*M*ove, damn you. *Move.*" Uff, stubborn animals. I nearly lost my balance trying to muscle my way through a trio of very large, very pink and hairy butts. When my mother brought an armful of squealing piglets to Meadowsong Farm, visions of savoring smoked bacon and slow-roasted pork shoulders filled my imagination, not hauling heavy buckets of feed and mucking pens daily.

Somewhere in the pigs' growth cycle, they'd gone from future food source to favored pet to four-hundred-pound behemoths. Nudging the closest meaty flank with my knee failed to produce the desired effect. I considered other ways to extricate myself from the holding pen.

You got yourself into this predicament, Maddie. You can get yourself out.

I snorted. My entire life from adolescence onward was a series of predicaments triggered by my need to find validation via physical affection. I turned over a new leaf the day my mother welcomed me onto her rambling farm in the middle of New Hampshire with a hug and a no-questions-asked policy. She'd directed the wide-eyed house elves clustered in the doorway behind her to air out one of the guest cabins, then pointed me toward the barn.

"Always something needs doing, Maddie. Don't be stubborn about wearing gloves to protect your hands," she'd cautioned. "Dinner bell rings at six. Leave your suitcase here."

Since arriving at Meadowsong, I'd learned that farming was exhausting work, leaving me little time for socializing. I didn't even try to keep up with my mother's boundless energy for everything gardening-related. Customers of her roadside stand often remarked on her "magic touch" with vegetables, flowers, and herbs. Mom would just smile and slip an extra pepper or heirloom apple or sample jar of relish into their bags.

Mom was fae and her inner source seemed to produce more magic as she aged, not less. I was half-fae, thanks to a human sperm donor, and had yet to uncap the well of magical potential the Queen of Optimism was convinced lay hidden inside my being. Moving in with her had been a last-ditch effort to save me from myself and my not-so-great habits of diving into relationships and schemes and hopping right out again.

That was ten months ago, and I hadn't had a lover or even a flirtation in all that time. Heck, I barely left the farm and when I did, it was only to run errands. Just as snow started to accumulate on my first full winter at Meadowsong Farm, I felt signs of restlessness surfacing. After dinner one night, while I jangled the keys to the truck and eyed the front door, my mother opened her laptop and beckoned me to her end of the table.

"My friend Habonde is advertising for apprentices," she said. "I think the two of you would get along."

I gawped at the photos of the Scottish Highlands, noted the presence of strapping men in beards and kilts and the lack of pigs, and applied. Today was the deadline to hear if I'd been accepted into the program. I'd buried myself—literally—in barn chores, thereby avoiding the rising sense I lacked some necessary trait for success and was forever doomed to be a chronically under-achieving, over-sexed, somewhat magical halfling.

The sudden trill of my phone startled the pigs and sent my heartbeat into overdrive. *This is it; this is it. Please, oh please, oh please, Goddess and Spirit and Chocolata and every other deity I bargained with on a regular basis, please let this be The Call.*

The phone rang again, urging me to act. I swung my pitchfork over the pen's waist-high dividing wall, then my right leg in its knee-high barn boot, and hopped atop the one-by-four. Damn if the board didn't hit me right in the lady-bits. I tugged off the heavy-duty work gloves and wedged them under my butt.

"Hello. Madeline Meadows here." I clenched my thighs like I was riding a horse. Better. Kind of.

"Madeline, this is Baubo Elefsina, Director of Programming for the Alliance of the Forgotten and Disremembered. You applied to enter our Goddess by Proxy training program."

Breathe in. Breathe out. Try to sound casual. "Oh, hi. Yes, I did."

"After careful review of your application and a conversation with your reference, our director, Habonde

Barleywine, has asked me to offer you a slot as a trainee."

Oh, thank you, thank you, thank you. Gripping the pitchfork handle, I swung my left leg over the wall and landed in a fragrant pile of fresh wood shavings. "I would be thrilled to accept."

Thrilled. Did that make me sound desperate?

"Excellent. I will send your welcome packet to the email address on file. Have a read-through as soon as you receive it and let me know if you have any questions."

I squeezed my eyes shut. A candidate confident of acceptance would have at least one question on the tip of their tongue.

Think, think.

Lightbulb! "When does the program begin?"

"March first." Baubo cleared her throat. "On a New Moon."

My knees wobbled and my back slid down the rough barnboards. Pigs snuffled on the other side of the wall. "March first of *next* year or this year?"

"This year."

"That's in two days," I noted helpfully.

"Is that a problem, Ms. Meadows?"

I bounced my forehead off my knees. Of course, it was a problem. I had to let my mother know she'd be down one farmhand, pack my things, and get myself all the way to Scotland. Booking a last-minute, one way flight was going to be an expensive proposition.

"No, not at all!"

"Well, then. Look for my email. Do you have any objections to portal travel?"

Sweet Abeona, guide my journey. I bit my forearm through the quilted flannel overshirt. Just hearing the word portal made me nauseous.

"None at all."

MY MOTHER RESPONDED to my news by insisting I deliver a picnic basket to Habonde crammed with fruit preserves, sundried tomatoes, and other goodies produced on Meadowsong Farm.

"Tell her Cleome La Fleur sends her regards."

"Cleome *LaFleur*?" I echoed, clearing a swath of snow off the porch with the side of my boot as we watched the bright green Broom car making its way up the winding driveway.

"Cleome LaFleur is my clan name."

"Do *I* have a clan name?" The driver scheduled to deliver me to Concord's portal station slowed to a stop at the bottom of the wide steps and lightly tapped the horn.

Mom chewed on her lower lip. "Mallow. Mallow La Fleur."

The trunk popped open, and the driver lowered their window. "Hello, Cleome. Need any help with the luggage?"

I raised my hand and spread my fingers. "Give us a minute. And yes, please load the carry-on and the picnic basket." I turned back to my mother. This was the first I was hearing of clan names. "Mallow? What kind of a name is *Mallow*?"

"Mallow, or *Malva sylvestris,* is a flower used extensively in herbal medicine. Every member of Clan LaFleur is named for a flower. I'm sure Habonde will include mallow in her classes on herbalogy and healing and you will see how much your namesake has to offer." My mother patted my back and urged me toward the car. "Go on now. Write me when you can. And Maddie?"

I swiped snow off the door handle and looked over my shoulder. "Yes?"

"I'm proud of you."

ELEVEN MONTHS LATER, after celebrating February first's Imbolc ritual with the other trainees, I found myself saying goodbye again. Leaving a place and a tightknit group of formerly lost souls like myself I'd grown to love was much harder than leaving Meadowsong Farm. But Habonde assured me I was ready to take on the duties of a proxy. I had passed my interview with Medusa who was, understandably, extremely eager to begin her year as a civilian.

It would be my job to care for her snakes, tend to her shrines, and uphold the Alliance of the Forgotten and Disremembered's primary mission of providing respite to the exhausted deities and mythological beings of pantheons all over this world and others.

Chapter Two

RHAIN BEAUCHÊNE

Clumps of slushy snow landed on my forearms. Eventually, every melting splotch would drizzle off the roughened surface of my marble skin to be funneled into the decorative waterspout clamped between my hands. Wet nights like this, when the tedium of being a gargoyle assigned to roof duty got to me, I imagined the pipe was my lover's flesh, not cold, unforgiving stone, and it was *my* release tumbling through the sky, not drops of—

"Got plans?" Owain, my next oldest brother and guardian of the rooftop corner nearest mine, interrupted my fantasy.

"Nope." I didn't bother returning the question. Owain always had plans, and those plans always included hooking up. He'd hook up with anyone. I bet if I shared my intimate thoughts on waterspouts, he'd say been there, done that, and laugh.

Now that the sky was dark enough for us to leave our corner perches, I released my grip and considered the night's options. How my ancestors had done this year after year after decade after century was beyond me. Even I tired of running a stream of sexual fantasies through my head as I monitored the sky and the streets and the buildings in an endless loop of watching, watching, and ever more watching.

To prevent Death by Boredom, I listened to podcasts for self-edification and audiobooks for entertainment. I'd even enrolled in online courses and was on my way to a second master's degree. Tedium aside, I had no idea what I wanted to do once this two-year contract was up, other than vacate Manhattan for a while, and find sexual partners willing to work around my unusual attributes.

My last in-person encounter had occurred the summer before I started this gig. After a few evenings of heavy flirting with a kitchen witch, I'd met up with her in the alley behind her Soho restaurant. Presented with an oddly shaped dick made of unfinished stone, she'd grabbed a pair of heavy-duty oven mitts and brought me close to getting off with an efficiency I found disheartening.

Immediately after tossing her mitts into a trash bin, the witch invited me to kneel and apply my tongue to her sex. While I derived satisfaction from her moans of pleasure, the apron she'd tossed over my face reminded me she, like others before her, found my visage difficult to gaze on for any length of time.

She didn't invite me to visit her back alley again. Which underscored my growing understanding that monsters like me weren't deserving of niceties like foreplay or aftercare.

At the corner diagonally across from mine, my oldest

brother shifted from stone to his flying form, rose out of a crouch, and stretched his wings. Like clockwork, the demon triplets of Jealousy, Longing, and Self-Doubt poked me in the ribs, reminding me the kitchen witch had spread her thighs only *after* she'd hidden my curved horns and forked tongue from sight—and that I would never fly.

Protected from human eyes by fae-made glamour, Daffyd leapt from his corner. I silently wished my favorite brother a good evening. He had demons of his own and deserved none of the envy I felt watching him simply living his life. He'd always been there for me, including during the aftermath of my first masturbatory experience.

I'd been a scrawny, curious thirteen-year-old. One day after school, I'd felt emboldened to experiment. I locked myself in my bedroom, clasped my hands around my dick, and found a rhythm and pressure that opened my eyes to a whole new world of possibilities.

The next thing I knew I was staring into Daffyd's face as he bit back his laughter.

"Dude, you can't do that," he said.

"Do what?" I fumbled to cover myself with the unzipped super-hero sleeping bag I preferred to sheets and blankets.

"Jerk off. I heard your bedsprings from the hall and waited until you finished. Only instead of a grunt, I heard you, y'know—" He mimed an explosion with his hands and added sound effects.

"So, you what, busted my door without my permission?"

"You're stone twenty-four-seven, little man, and I guess it's my job to let you know that every time you have an orgasm, you're going to fall apart. As in literally Fall. Apart." He stretched out his arm and swiped something off my desk. "Here's what you looked like, jizz and all."

He held his magic hand-mirror to face me. Squinting, I absorbed the startling implications of pebbles and body-shaped pieces of stone littering the top of the sheet. Smack in the middle were fisted hands. And a six-inch obelisk. And a wet spot.

At least my dick didn't break.

I prayed for the mattress to swallow me whole. My brother nudged me with his knee. "You're embarrassed, I know, and I should have told you sooner."

"Told me what?"

"That you never, *ever* play with yourself when you're stone and alone."

"But what if I wasn't alone?" Real sex with a real being was high on the list of things I knew I wanted to try.

"Then whoever you're with has to know the spell that keeps you bound so this" —he waggled his device in my face— "never happens again."

"So, like, another gargoyle?"

My brother nodded, adding, "If it turns out you're into guys."

Gargoyles were always male. Though I didn't yet know enough about who I was and what I wanted to yay or nay the idea of having sex with other guys, the idea didn't freak me out.

Breaking into pieces without anyone around to put me back together did.

"How'd you fix me?"

My brother lowered his forehead to his hand and

sighed. "If you break all the way, whoever you're with has to lay the pieces of stone as close to each other as they can and then speak a specific spell."

I swallowed hard. That meant my brother had—

"Yeah, yeah, I touched your junk. Don't make me do it again."

"Thanks. I'm glad it was you, not Owain or Trey." Daffyd was cool. And he could keep a secret. Owain worshiped at the shrine of assholery and Trey was only ten.

"I'll teach you the spell," he continued. "You should probably memorize it and share it with anyone you plan on having sex with." He grinned and scuffed his knuckles roughly over my head. "But wait a few years, okay?"

That incident occurred almost twenty years ago. To be on the safe side, I had the reconstruction spell carved into my forearms once I turned sixteen and asked a friend apprenticing with a jeweler to inlay the grooves with rose gold and rubies. I didn't bleed when my carapace cracked and for whatever reason, teenage me wanted to pretend I could. Made me feel more human. Still did.

The pale flash of a lamp coming on drew my attention to the building across the side street. The northeast-facing condo on the Belleport's fifth floor had undergone months of renovations during the fall and early winter and been dark since mid-January. Pushing sleet off my forearms, I homed in on the figure now moving through the room and waited for them to pull the curtains apart and gaze out over their new neighborhood.

Every human performed the same, predictable ritual when they first moved in and this one was no exception.

Like so many others, this one shook out her thick locks, planted her hands on the window's interior sill, and rested her forehead on the glass.

And then her head exploded, sending percussive echoes right into my chest. I had to call 9-1-1, or alert someone inside the Belleport or the shifters in my building's lobby. The woman needed *help*.

Gripping the outer lip of the balustrade, I peered into the window more closely. She didn't seem to need medical help. Magical help was more like it. Her bald head remained intact atop her neck while sections of her hair flowed along the glass in all directions, like black rays from a darkened sun. The snaky pieces stopped moving. The woman reached behind to undo her dress, shrugged the straps over her shoulders, and jerked the garment down her body.

It was a good thing I'd taken a seat on the narrow stone wall ringing the roof. The curving shapes on the inside of the window peeled away and returned to their nearly naked mistress. Taking a step back from the expanse of glass, she opened her arms wide as if waiting for her lover's embrace and left the room.

Melting snow drizzled down my forehead. I stopped thinking I should call for help and opened myself to the possibility the woman in 5A might be someone I should get to know.

Oh, it was a relief beyond measure to be *home*, even though the newly renovated condo I'd splurged on was barely furnished. The movers placed my king-sized mattress and a floor lamp in the spacious master bedroom, and the fancy, French baroque table in the oval-shaped foyer. The gilt-edged piece, also oval-shaped, turned out to be too big to use as a bedside table. Luckily, it functioned perfectly as a place to drop my purse and keys, with enough room for hat forms and pincushion. Alopecia claimed my hair years ago and when I went out, I either went bald, or big.

Showing up to the Kentucky Derby in full regalia was just one of my dreams.

Back in reality, boxes of items to outfit my kitchen lined the short hall, waiting to be unpacked, plugged in, and put away. Four reusable cloth shopping bags stood side-by-side on the kitchen counter. I'd asked the Belleport's concierge to have the local grocer deliver an order of basics. I quickly stashed the perishables in the refrigerator, then filled the ridiculously expensive crystal vase I'd bought on a whim with cold tap water, a crushed aspirin, and the fresh flowers I'd carefully set in the sink.

I'd bought an armful, not a few discounted stems; not a tired, cellophane-wrapped bundle wilting by the checkout counter; an *armful*. I specified to the neighborhood's hoity-toity florist I wanted white flowers, no roses, and I got white flowers, with hypnotic names like lisianthus, jessamine, agapanthus, and veronica. The accompanying stems of greenery were the *fancy* kind I could never afford to pay for until now.

Between the furniture, the flowers, the specialty appliances, and high thread-count sheets, I'd never spent so much money on myself in such a short amount of time. The contents of the bags of beauty products waiting in the bathroom would alone have broken the Maddie Meadows Bank two years ago.

I carried the heavy vase in and out of every room of my home—my *home!*—and ended up placing it atop the ormolu table beside the clawfoot tub in my bedroom's en suite. Before I could choose a bathe oil, or have my dinner, I had the snakes to care for. All venomous seven of them, each with their own personalities and needs, and all inclined to dither over whose tails would twine beneath my chin to keep them from sliding off my head.

As soon as Medusa's snakes had been entrusted to my care, I realized the creatures were both a blessing and a curse. I couldn't neglect them or even hand them over to someone, because forgetting to feed and handle the serpents in addition to wearing them on my head meant giving up a steady paycheck, a series of ever-increasing bonuses, *and* refreshed magical powers.

After I completed my current contract, I would return the snakes to their rightful mistress. I would never, however, return to my old ways and I would never, *ever* underestimate, under-use, or deny my rural fae magic again, not for anyone.

Okay, Maddie, time for a reality check.

I chuffed out a breath and lowered my expectations. I would try my best to avoid resuming past not-so-great habits, which mostly revolved around physical intimacy. The deal Habonde brokered included a clause preventing me from having a lover for the entire year of my contract. I'd taken a hard look at my life and decided I could live with that restriction. Sex toys and streamers broadcasting from their home bedrooms would appease my libido and keep me out of trouble.

To be on the safe side, I had asked Habonde if self-pleasuring was okay. She shared her "one-a-day" rule. Medusa must have overhead us talking because she included a marble dildo in the welcome basket she sent to the Belleport. The object was old, and likely a joke, but something about the partial fig leaf at its base rang a bell. An internet search confirmed my suspicion.

I was in possession of an antiquity.

Which was illegal.

On a meticulously pre-planned visit to the Metropolitan Museum of Art, I dropped the dildo in the donation box, where it disappeared into a cushion of fives, tens, and twenties. I hadn't returned to the museum since.

Flowers delivered, I wandered into to my bedroom and took hold of the semi-sheer curtains blocking my view of the mansion across the street.

"We're home, girls," I whispered, spreading my arms and lowering my forehead to the window's cool surface. The restless little monsters sprung off my head like I'd blown a starter's whistle and crawled across the broad expanse of glass to get away from one another. Laughing at their antics, I unzipped my dress, shimmied it down my legs, and admired my reflection.

Goddess and Spirit, I was so damn horny. Today's lingerie set deserved an appreciative audience and thinking about dildos reminded me how much I missed connecting skin-to-skin and face-to-face. Blessed Hedone, I missed face-to-ass, face-to-the-pillow and ass-in-the-air and every other combination two bodies and more could get into. Unfortunately, succumbing to my longing for physical intimacy would negate my contract and that was a very, *very* high price to pay for a fuck.

Le sigh. I could do this. I *would* do this. February first meant I was in the home stretch, and once I crossed the finish line on the twenty-eighth, I was free to pursue whomever and whatever I wanted. Horniness aside, New York City's endless supply of galleries and museums and artists had worked their magic on my imagination, showing me that when I wasn't chasing sex, I had more energy to chase my dream of becoming a sculptor.

A sculpt*ress*. Yes, "sculptress" carried just the right amount of European flair. To move myself closer to my goal, I'd enrolled in two courses at the Academy of Art: Life Drawing, and Sculpting in Stone. One month in, my creative juices were flowing, and I'd been accepted at a prestigious art school. Those classes would start in September.

For the first time in my adult life, I could afford to be a full-time student.

My sigh echoed through the mostly empty room. Once I'd tasted the rewards of Habonde's training program, I'd set the bar high after years of setting it so low it was practically subterranean.

I wanted a classy address in a posh neighborhood. I found it at the Belleport, which I chose because it both fit the bill *and* I'd seen dragons landing on the roof across the street when the real estate broker walked me through this very unit.

Yep, *dragons*. Enhanced fae magic meant I could see the glamours Magicals used to mask their presence. Lore stated proximity to dragons meant proximity to the finest material things in life, and I aspired to finer things. My broker's offhand remark there was an art gallery in the dragons' mansion sealed the deal.

Fire-breathing Magicals hoarding gold and jewels, *and* art?

Sold.

I would introduce myself to the Winslows soon. For now, I needed to put the snakes to bed, pour myself a glass of the young sauternes that was on my tasting list, and draw a bath.

My giggling teetered on the verge of hysteria. Who the heck said, "Draw a bath?" and who was I to imagine myself a fancy-pants pretend heiress and future *sculptress*? What I really was, was a quarry pond princess who'd cut a deal with a big-wig mythological creature in need of a break. I kicked off my high heels before I twisted an ankle and set to tending the snakes.

LATER, after musing on my future as I stood at the kitchen counter eating take-out pad thai, I looked in on the girls. Each was asleep in their own padded hat box, happily curled around their favorite stuffies. Securing the mesh lids, I whispered goodnight. Not one of them stirred. I imagined they were feeling somewhat lazy from their fresh field mouse dinner; that, and the warmth seeping up from the guest bathroom's heated tile floor. I could safely leave them to digest right where they were for the next twenty-four hours.

My scalp started itching in response to the thought of not wearing the snakes for a day. Leaving the night-light on and the door ajar, I refreshed my wine glass from the open bottle in the kitchen and surveyed the primary room of my domain, with its large rectangular window and the view to the roof of the dragon's four-story mansion.

There, elaborately carved gargoyles connected by a low stone wall guarded the two corners facing me. A wrought-iron fence loomed behind the imposing figures and on the other side of the fence I spied what looked like an outdoor sitting area.

Turning off the lamp beside my bed, I waited for my eyes to adjust to the dark. Patches of snow coated the gargoyles' shoulders and heads. Potted trees, wrapped for the winter and decorated with tiny lights, twinkled in the gloom. For a moment, I missed the fireflies that lit up the fields on summer nights at Meadowsong.

But home was no longer the farm, home was New York City, and I was no longer filling orders for fried fish and chips out the side of a food truck, or chasing chickens and pigs and putting up wheelbarrows full of zucchini and tomatoes.

Mesmerized by the decorative outdoor lights, I twitched when they suddenly shut off, then promptly made a mental note to order some for my bedroom. I continued to relax, sipping the sweet wine and savoring the added extras my credit card provided.

"You take care of my snakes and I'll take care of you," was how Medusa put it. Her occasional texts radiated relief that her darlings were in excellent hands. Plus, being unburdened of a reputation of mythological proportions meant she was finally able to more fully explore the single life.

Feeling quieted and ready for sleep, I kicked off the covers. My toes curled on the cold wooden floor as I padded down the hall. I wanted to check on the girls one more time, brush my teeth, and re-engage the bolts on the front door. Satisfied all was well, I jumped back into bed, bounced on my knees, and stopped.

The gargoyle closest to me had gone from squatting to standing on the edge of the building—*standing!*—and now he was stretching. Illuminated by a skyward-pointing spotlight, he turned to one side, and the other, and I sucked in a breath. His magnificent semi-erection pointed due east, then due west. At least, I *thought* that's what I saw. Though it could have been the pommel of a sword or a tennis racket handle. Squinting, I looked again. Yep, Stone Man sported a woodie. Or a stonie. Aroused, I sat back on my heels, rucked up my T-shirt, and wedged my hands between my thighs.

The creature stroked himself once, twice. Oh, the heck with those little lights, I was buying *binoculars*. Tomorrow. The monster's eyes glowed—I couldn't discern the color from so far away—and he slowly tilted his head to the left, then to the right. I thought he was settling back in, until he lifted his chin slightly and looked straight at me. I held my breath. Eased up on the tension in my legs. This was more intimate, more *arousing*, than my usual voyeuristic video fare. I kept my gaze on him, and he kept his on me. With one hand tweaking my nipple, I sneakily stroked myself into a surprisingly fast release.

Another gargoyle joined the object of my attention as my vision cleared. At least, I thought it was a gargoyle. The two talked and then my guy hit the other guy, and the second gargoyle stomped off.

My guy resumed staring. One of his eyes blinked. Was he *winking* at me? Was that quirk in the side of his mouth a...a *smirk*? He took hold of the erection I'd admired minutes ago. He didn't move, didn't stroke himself into a reciprocal release, he just stood there until faster than a darter fish escaping a frog's tongue, he opened the gate to the fire escape and disappeared.

Chapter Four

RHAIN BEAUCHÊNE

The minx in the building across the street had her eyes on me and I didn't mind. I only minded that no matter what fantasy I conjured or how much the thought of meeting her aroused me, "we" had nowhere to go.

Owain propped his elbow on my shoulder. He assumed his horn-free human form every other night and stayed in its skin as long as he could.

"Still plotting your opening line?" His voice was smooth as silk and annoying as fuck. "You've been watching that sweet piece across the street since she moved in. Why don't you see if she has a cup of sugar you can borrow? You could tell her you're in the mood for cupcakes. Or if you're afraid she'll freak out, I could ask her." He gave a low laugh. "In fact, I think I'll go over there right now and ring her bell. Maybe use my little brother's sob story to get laid. 'Hi, my name's Rhain. I'm cursed to wear this face forever. Do you think you could ever love me?'"

I made a fist and punched Owain in the ribs. Something cracked, and it wasn't my stone skin.

"What the f—"

"You know what? You're an ass," I said. "The Belleport's mine to watch, it's in our agreement with the Winslows, so keep your hands off the building *and* its occupants." I crossed my arms and stared at the darkened window. *Especially her.* Because now that Owain was interested, meeting the neighbor across the street had become imperative.

"And you're afraid, Micah Rhain. Get the fuck over yourself and for once in your life, go for what you want." He held his ribs as he followed the narrow walkway to the fire escape stairs. "Because if you don't, I will."

I had to leave the roof after that interaction. Trey was fully healed from his last mission, and it was his night to watch the backside of the mansion anyway. I got as far as crossing the side street between the Winslow's and the Belleport before I acknowledged what I was doing. I'd told myself I wanted to check the safety and accessibility of the other building's fire escape. In reality, I wanted to catch the mystery woman's scent.

Grateful for the freedom provided by my fae-made glamour, I scoured the alleyway, searching for lights on the fifth floor. Every window was dark and the pulley for the metal stairs was locked tight, as it should have been. Doubling back, I took the side street to Park Avenue and slowed as I rounded the corner.

Flowers. A mélange of floral residue assaulted my nostrils and I sneezed, startling the trio of Shiba Inus exiting the double doors. Their exasperated owner followed close behind, arm extended by the straining leashes, ready to dress down whomever was responsible for their dogs freaking out. I slipped inside the building in the ensuing commotion and followed my nose through the lobby, past the middle-aged man chatting on a land-line phone, and into the elevator.

The lingering smell of flowers was stronger here. Lack of a key thwarted my desire to explore further. I exited the elevator, skirted the desk, and paused to eavesdrop on the concierge.

"Thank you for the compliment, Ms. Meadows. I am delighted to hear everything arrived. If there is anything else you—" The man paused, raised both eyebrows, and woke the screen on his tablet. "I know we have several excellent veterinarians in the area, but did I hear correctly you need one that handles exotic pets? What kind of exotic pets may I ask?"

He blanched, then quickly recovered. I found his discomfort entertaining. "Snakes. I see." He nodded along with whatever this Ms. Meadows was saying. "It reassures me to hear your girls adore their housing arrangements and would never want to escape. More than one of your fellow residents has said the same thing about life here at the Belleport. I shall have a list of herpetological special-ists sent up to you in the morning. Good night to you too, Ms. Meadows."

Georges, according to his name tag, hung up and punched in another number. "Désirée? The new owner of 5A has brought *snakes* with her." He paused. "I agree it could be worse. It could be ferrets. Or chihuahuas. I'm preparing a list of veterinarians, which I will leave at the front desk. Deliver it to her in the morning along with her packages. She tips *exceedingly* well and she's rather a darling. Almost like she's overcompensating for something. I'm sure you'll have her story figured out in no time."

He ended the call, then planted his hands on the desk and stared at the door. "Snakes in the Belleport," he muttered under his breath. "Next, she'll invite those lizards over for tea."

I hesitated. If Georges knew enough about the gharial shifters employed by the Winslows to call them "lizards," he had to be a Magical. Pleased with my information gathering, I exited the building and crossed Park Avenue. Underneath my stone skin everything felt agitated and slightly electrified. My best option was to run it off while plotting how I was going to introduce myself to the mysterious Ms. Meadows.

I COMPLETED my run at the Winslow's front entrance. Kunal, one of the gharial shifters working the lobby, was on duty. I dropped my glamour once I stepped into the alcove near the front desk and relayed what I'd overheard at the Belleport.

"You thought Georges was a Magical like *us*?" he asked, crossing his arms as I finished.

"He's not a gharial and he's definitely not a gargoyle."

Kunal scuffed the polished floor with the toe of his shoe. "I know for a fact both Georges and Désirée are human."

"Then how do they know about you and Tan and Aravind?"

"They belong to a group of 'Observationalists.' As far as I can tell, they're harmless. All they do is watch their area for evidence of pheromonic activity, write their reports, and occasionally have these...get-togethers. Tea and scones and big hats, that sort of thing."

"Oh. Huh." I shrugged. "So, I can walk into the Belleport like this, and they won't freak out?"

Kunal guffawed as I attempted a catwalk between the desk and the entrance to the art gallery. "Sure, if you want their heads to explode," he said, swiping the corners of his eyes. "What were you doing over there in the first place?"

"Following the scent of a woman." I turned, miming a man overcome with love. "Or at least the fresh flowers she brought into the building."

Kunal nodded knowingly. We'd traded life stories bit by bit over the past year and were privy to each other's dreams and challenges. "I hope you get to meet her one day."

"Me too."

Chapter Five

MADDIE MEADOWS

My first Sunday morning in my new home finally arrived. I stayed in bed as long as I could, leaving the cushy mattress once to open the blackout shades on the big window so I could ogle my gargoyle pal through the raindrops, and again to make myself a cup of cocoa. Sipping and staring at the rooftop across the way, I listened for tell-tale rustlings over the baby monitor. The snakes were due to go back on my head, which normally I wouldn't dread. Except the girls had grown increasingly ornery over the past week, nipping at each other and shaking their tails.

Maybe the move from Habonde's sanctuary to Manhattan had made them anxious. Or maybe they needed nookie as much as I did. My proxy training hadn't covered the sex lives of snakes. Giggling, I texted Medusa to see if she was available. Moments later, my phone buzzed, lighting up with a series of raindrop emojis. I assumed she was taking advantage of the weekend, too, except *she* had company.

>*Sorry for interrupting,* I wrote.

>>*The only thing you are interrupting is the last of the afterglow,* she replied. *Is something wrong?*

>*The snakes are cranky, and I was wondering if you had any suggestions for how I could cheer them up.*

>>*They don't do well in winter, especially when the weather is unsettled.*

>*We've had nothing but sleet and snow.*

>>*My poor darlings. Have you had any handsome visitors? Any flirtations? Taken the girls with you on a date?*

>*Uh, no. None of the above. I took Habonde's warning srsly!!!* A single emoji popped up, this one the tear-streaked laugh. I responded with, *There's nothing funny about cranky snakes!*

>>*Then make sure to take them outside on the next sunny day. Ta!*

More drops splattered against the window, affirming it was *still* lousy and giving me an idea. I slipped from my warm bed and stood as close to the big pane of glass as I could. Holding the hem of my T-shirt, I performed a daytime striptease for my gargoyle, balancing on tiptoes to show off a pair of sheer lace panties before revealing my breasts. The air was cold enough to harden my nipples. Feeling daring, I pressed my chest and the side of my face against the glass and imagined my mystery monster entering me from behind.

Oh Goddess, the sharp cold shouldn't have felt so good, but it did. I slipped my fingers between my thighs and swirled my own natural lubricant around my clit. I imagined pressing my ass against the gargoyle's stony exterior, the contrast of my warmth enfolding his cool, rock-hard cock, and rubbed one off right then and there.

I kept my eyes open, even though the roof across the way was barely visible in my peripheral vision. Recovering from the high of orgasming, I noticed I'd steamed up the inside of the window, leaving the faint but unmistakable impression of my cheek, breasts, and belly for anyone to see. I darted into the kitchen to wash my hands, then swiped the linen dishtowel across the glass, smudging the surface as I erased the evidence of what I'd done. I couldn't see my gargoyle nearly as well, which sent a swell of loneliness up through my chest.

Tears stung my eyes. What the—? Hand shaking, I wiped my cheeks with the dishtowel and noticed sounds coming from the baby monitor.

"Coming, coming," I yelled, in response to the girls slithering in circles inside their hatboxes. I found a pair of leggings and a sleeveless T-shirt in the basket of unfolded laundry in my closet and shoved my arms into a flannel shirt. I knew from experience I had less than a minute before one of the snakes would have a dramatic meltdown and trigger her sisters into one-upping each other.

Folding the bathmat underneath my knees, I quickly lifted the lids and invited my charges onto my arms one at a time. They'd never been so bitchy before, and I had to intervene multiple times until the seven were settled.

If they continued to get moodier and moodier, I would get nothing done. I raised the volume on their favorite jazz station. That didn't help. I turned the music off and headed to the kitchen. Opening the tablet I kept propped on the counter, I searched for a movie or documentary. As with little kids, the snakes would sit still if the right show was on. I found a nature program, turned up the volume, and reached for the refrigerator. The two tails looped under my chin tightened their grip, making it hard to swallow.

"Vassar. Radcliffe. Cut it out." I'd named the seven asps after the Seven Sisters—the women's colleges, not the star cluster—and as I wedged my fingers between my throat and the knot, pinpricks of light burst across my vision.

I'M NOT sure what happened next. I came to face up on the floor near the gilt table in the foyer. Rolling to my side, I patted my cheeks and unoccupied scalp and scanned my body. Everything was intact and unviolated. Though my head was woozy and the snakes were gone.

The snakes were *gone*. Oh Goddess, oh Goddess, I was in a fuckton of trouble if they had escaped the Belleport or worse, been kidnapped. Getting to my knees, I felt around the top of the oval table and found my phone.

I had no one I could call. No, wait. The day after I moved in, I'd contacted Habonde and asked her to fill me in on the Winslows and the gargoyles. Turns out Mr. Chunky and Hunky and his brothers were hired guards known as the Watchers.

Clutching my phone, I crawled toward my bedroom on wobbly hands and knees. Outside the big window, what little I could see of the sky was painted with streaks of purple and lights were coming on in the nearby buildings. My stomach growled. Had I managed to make myself something to eat? And why had I collapsed in the foyer, not the kitchen?

I sat on my butt and blinked my eyes. *Look for the snakes, Maddie. Solve the mystery later.* Scrambling to my feet, I tore down the hall to the guest bedroom suite, yelled for the bathroom lights to come on, and widened the door.

The seven hat boxes were just as I'd left them: three on one side, four on the other, lids propped open. I peeked inside the closest one. Empty. Heart pounding, I discovered all seven snakes curled together in the furthest box. Relief shuddered through my body. In my eleven-plus months as Medusa's proxy, I'd never felt more like I needed a friend.

I covered the occupied hatbox, carried it to the kitchen, and set it on the counter. Grabbing a black marker, I scrawled HELP across the back of the large white envelope containing the refrigerator's warranty and pressed my message to the narrow window over the sink. The gargoyle with a thing for my windows might be waiting for more boob flashes.

Hunky made no sign he'd seen my plea. Then again, when I wanted his attention I usually stood in front of the window in my bedroom. Clicking my fingers, I waved my flaming fingertips back and forth in front of the wide span of glass. My gargoyle raised his arm in acknowledgment and disappeared down the backside of his building.

Okie dokie. Either he was running toward me, or away. I doused the flames, returned to the kitchen, and tossed the warranty packet on the counter. Moments later, I heard a succinct *tap-tap-tap* on one of the rear-facing windows in the far side of my unit.

I curled my arms around the heavy hatbox. "Lights on full."

My condo blazed. I stomped down the hall and into my future studio. Only, I couldn't see out. "Lights off."

Better. The gargoyle crouching on the metal fire escape took my breath away. Fierce horns swept back from his hairline and his mottled, stony skin blended with every other sleet-covered thing. Up close, separated by double-paned windows, I wasn't sure which of us was the observer and which was the observed.

"You need help?" he asked.

Blessed Hedone, I was in all kinds of trouble. Because that *voice*. Deep, gravelly, and close enough to my favorite ASMR announcer's resonant timbre that I soaked my panties on the spot and the girls stirred against the hatbox's papered-over cardboard interior.

Twenty-three more days before you can fuck, Maddie Meadows. Twenty-three more days.

Forcing my jelly-jointed legs to propel me across the empty room, I set down the hatbox, flicked the locks, and lifted the lower sash.

"I'm Maddie." I stepped back and invited the gargoyle in. He moved gracefully for someone wearing a coating of stone and made a point of keeping his limbs from marring the painted wood. As soon as he was inside, he closed and locked the window.

"Rhain Beauchêne." Rhain had a faintly Welsh accent. Color me dead and gone. I held onto the hand he'd offered and savored the novelty of feeling like a delicate, vulnerable bird cradled in a big stone nest.

This little bird fluffed up her chest. "You've been watching me."

"Yes, I have. Monitoring activity in this building and others in the vicinity is in my contract with the Winslows and technically, you're part of this building."

"I did my own research. I know fae-made glamours shield you and the other gargoyles." I tried to not fall forward into his arms as he gently released my hand. "I'm fae, by the way," I added. "Half-fae."

"I'm all gargoyle." He swept his hand down the front of his body, which of course made me look at the perfection of his torso and the outline of his uncut—oh my, his *literally* uncut—cock underneath his sweats. If I could take my stone polishing tools to *that* I'd have him smoothed to pleasurable perfection in no time.

Widening his stance, he held his hands in front of his crotch military-style, ending my shameless appraisal. Good thing, as I was about to embarrass myself by drooling.

"Now, tell me why you want my help."

"I—" I tried to keep my cool, I really did, but hearing his name inside my head conjured images of Medusa's water drop emoji and me coming on his face and I forgot how to use words.

Rhain tilted his head to the side. I had to fire up my language center and decide how much to share. "I'm a caretaker for a nest of snakes that belong to a VIP client. *Very* VIP," I blurted, in typical Maddie Shares All-style. "This morning, after I got up and—"

"And flashed your breasts at me?" My cheeks flamed like briquets under a stream of lighter fluid, which sent the gargoyle chortling. "Hey, if getting a rise out of me helps you get up in the morning, flash away." He coughed into his fist. "I interrupted you. Please, continue."

"I got dressed, got the snakes settled on top of my head, and opened the refrigerator door." I mimed the movement. "Oh, and I remember feeling like I was choking. The girls were cranky this morning and they were holding onto my neck extra tight."

Rhain tipped my chin up with his knuckle and stepped closer to examine my throat. "Hmm, I don't see any bruising or ligature marks. How are the snakes now?"

"They're in there and they're fine." I pointed to the hatbox. "I was too freaked out to do a thorough search of the rest of my condo and that's when I reached out to you."

Did I go bold and tell him the truth, that my misfortune provided the perfect opportunity to get close enough to him I could assess my chances of enjoying more than long-distance looks? Because since moving in, I'd spent a lot of hours trying and failing to come up with a convincing reason to visit the Winslow's roof.

Staring into his eyes, I leaned into my shy country mouse persona. "I'm very new in town and aside from the Belleport staff, I don't know anyone."

Rhain shifted his weight. Ambient light from outside shimmered across the facets of his rough skin. Watching him was like watching an unfinished sculpture come to life.

"Would you feel better if I walked through your home with you?"

"I would. Very much. Lead the way." And don't mind me staring at your ass muscles. Which I was supposed to be doing anyways for my Life Drawing class. I hefted the hatbox and stepped aside. The gargoyle hesitated.

"I examined the fire escape as I made my way up," he admitted, "and I can take a look at the roof later."

I followed him closely as he opened closet doors and felt along walls and into corners. "Do you know any creatures that can go invisible?"

"Phantoms. Will-o-wisps. Any Magical with the right connections and enough cash can buy a decent fae-made glamour. We done in here?" At my nod, he stepped into the hall. I pointed toward the semi-oval foyer with the oval table, pleased with my initial attempts at decorating my new home.

"This is where I woke up." I stopped thinking about what Rhain's body might look like when he wasn't covered in stone, undid the lock and deadbolt, and opened the front door to a quiet, empty vestibule.

Rhain went to one knee, steadying himself on his fingertips and sniffing the air. Goddess, he took up a lot of space and he moved as though he knew it, keeping his arms tucked in and all. What would it take for him to move with abandon, to just…dance?

He straightened and settled his back against the opposite wall. I'd noticed the flocked wallpaper here and in the ground floor lobby before, but it hadn't called for a closer look until now. With curlicues of ferns and flowers forming a background of vertical stripes, Rhain was the embodiment of Pan, with his elegant horns and carved curls of short, wavy hair.

I wanted to sculpt the gargoyle just as he was, in the worst way. I curled my handsy fingers into fists and stared boldly.

Twenty-three days, Maddie Meadows. Twenty-three days.

"Let me show you the rest of the rooms." Goddess and Spirit, let me not lead him into temptation.

Chapter Six

RHAIN BEAUCHÊNE

Maddie ducked into one of the bathrooms and settled her snakes. Closing the door, she led me through her Park Avenue-facing living room, the open concept kitchen and dining area, and into the master bedroom. I could have lingered there, offered suggestions for tweaking the placement of the bed to afford me optimal views of her as she slept, or self-pleasured. She hurried me out, and into the wide hall bisecting the condo.

At the end of the hall, she paused before a set of double doors. "This was supposed to be the master bedroom. It's got a massive en suite and walk-in closet." She turned the handles and pushed. "I decided to turn it into a studio. Lights on."

The bulbs on the modest chandelier suspended from the center of the ceiling brightened.

"I'm not sure what to do about the floor," she said, suddenly nervous. "I had the maple boards refinished before I knew I wasn't going to sleep in here. For now, I installed those dense pieces of foam, you know, the kinds they use in gyms? I didn't want to drop a tool and put a dent in the wood."

"I've never been to a gym, but I know what you mean. Might be good to top the padding with tarps to protect from dust and moisture. All depends on what materials you plan on using."

I left her side and zeroed in on the worktable, where mallets and hammers and whet stones lay sorted into straight lines. The bulk of Maddie's smaller sculpting tools lay in a jumble on her worktable. I inserted my finger into the pile and nudged apart rifflers, rasps, and chisels. A diamond "S" file caught my eye, and I wondered how it would feel to have Maddie draw the tool against my skin.

"I work primarily in stone." She came up beside me and ran her finger along the smooth edge of the curved file. My heartbeat pounded in my ears. The scent of her arousal rose above the faint smell of flowers I'd earlier encountered in the lobby.

I could have stayed exactly as we were until we'd traded life stories and gotten to the important stuff, like our obvious mutual attraction. I set the "S" file on the table and cleared my throat, Owain's challenge ringing in my ears.

"You want to touch me, don't you?"

"I do," she whispered, pulling her arms behind her back. "But I wasn't going to ask." She darted a glance up at me. "You must get sick of people asking. Or touching you without permission."

"The only people I see on a regular basis are my brothers, the family that owns the mansion, and the Magicals who work for them. They're all pretty used to how I look."

"I get sick of being asked about this," she said, waving a hand over her bald head. "Guys especially think they're being funny when they ask if I'm bald 'everywhere'," she added, crooking her fingers into quotation marks.

Like those bar room idiots, I was curious too. Only, I wasn't going to ask. I was going to find out by process of eliminating her clothes, one piece at a time. Patting the top of the nearest stool, I asked, "Mind if I sit?"

"Be my guest."

I picked up both stools and placed them closer to the worktable. I had to adjust myself underneath the loose running pants I'd zipped myself into at the bottom of her fire escape before I could sit comfortably.

"Have a seat."

"Wh-where?"

"On the other stool," I said, gentling my voice. As much as I wanted Maddie on my lap, I didn't want to damage her skin. She tucked the back of her flannel shirt under her butt and sat. I offered up my palm. "You can see my skin's worn down in a few places."

She placed her palm atop mine, tentative and light before stroking me with her fingers. The corners of her mouth lifted. "Feels like you work a lot with your hands."

"I did. I mean, I do. I must, to keep the texture smooth. Otherwise, the minerals in the stone re-form over time."

"Those sparkly veins are pretty." I followed the path of her light brown eyes, allowing me to fully appreciate the artistry of her winged eyeliner.

"Sparkly?" I wasn't sure what she meant. I was

distracted by the way her shirt was falling off one shoulder. She traced the rose gold inlays on my inner forearms. "Oh, those aren't veins, they're the words to a spell."

"What kind of spell?"

"The spell someone has to speak as I'm orgasming. If they don't, or I can't, I—" Wow, talk about a now or never situation. "If the spell isn't activated, I fall apart after I orgasm. Which means whomever I'm with has to speak it in order for all of my pieces to reassemble."

"Your *pieces*?"

"When I orgasm, it's no *petit mort*," I joked. I didn't know why I suddenly thought I should disguise the severity of my situation with humor and fancy language.

"What's petit—?" Maddie's mouth opened in surprise and her lips formed a small "O."

"Would you like to hear my story?"

"I want you to tell me whatever you're comfortable sharing. I don't know much about gargoyles, other than you have three forms."

"That's mostly true. However, the me you see is the only me you're going to get. I had a run-in with a witch and her wand when we were both kids. I've looked like this ever since, despite my mother's efforts to reverse the spell." I gave Maddie a minute to let that sink in. "Most gargoyles are immobile in their stone form. I have a stone skin. I can run and stretch and make most movements the human body can, and if a piece of this skin cracks and breaks off, it re-grows."

"What about bodily fluids?"

"Like blood?"

"Like blood. Sweat. Saliva. Semen."

"My body produces versions of all those, except for sweat." Though it felt like I was sweating now. Underneath my skin, my temperature rose, and the angle of my erection started to feel uncomfortable.

"You okay?" Maddie asked, examining my face. "Your jaw's twitching."

I uncrossed my legs. Slipping my hand under my waistband, I made a necessary adjustment. And made it again just so I could watch her eyes follow the movement of my hand.

"May I see what you have in there?"

I hesitated, surprised at the bluntness of Maddie's huskily whispered request. "I don't look like other men."

"Why don't you let me be the judge of that?"

Holding my breath, I leaned back, gingerly setting my elbows on the worktable. Maddie slid off her stool and stepped between my thighs. I felt...bulky. Monstrous. She braced one hand on my shoulder, then took hold of my waistband and pulled it toward her and down, wedging my dick in place. She mouthed a silent, *wow,* before speaking.

"You're right. You're *not* built like other men."

She pondered the obelisk angled against my belly. At least it had a normal-ish looking head, rather than a multi-sided point. Maddie leaned to one side, and the other, before drumming her fingertips against her lips. "I am simultaneously aroused and terrified. How— how do you fit inside someone?"

Fine cracks split the skin on my cheeks. Shame mixed with anger heated my underskin. "I don't. I mean, I haven't. Not completely."

Maddie used both hands to stretch the waistband underneath my sack. She scrunched up her face like I was a problem needing solving. "What if I, if *we*, could do something about this?"

"I'm listening."

"How is your pain threshold?"

No one had ever asked me *that* before. "My *pain* threshold?"

Maddie reached past me, to the table at my back and the line-up of tools. "See this?" she asked, waving the curved file in the air. "I might be able to make it possible for you to comfortably insert yourself into another body in the usual orifices. Using a good lubricant, of course."

I knew Maddie's matter-of-fact approach meant her offer came from a place of genuinely wanting to help. But she was waving a diamond dust-encrusted tool inches from my dick while pondering how to sand off its edges and the whole thing struck me as absurdly funny.

I laughed. She pouted and looked a little miffed. "'The usual orifices'?" I quoted, lifting her chin with my knuckle so we could see eye to eye.

"I only meant— I was just trying to be—" Maddie gave up reaching for an explanation and started giggling. "Oh, my Goddess," she gasped, "you crack me up."

Chapter Seven

RHAIN BEAUCHÊNE

B oth of us laughing only made things worse. I had to nudge Maddie's hands off my running pants and cover myself out of fear she'd bump against me and injure herself. Or worse, that I'd accidentally mar her skin. Though the offer to take her tools to mine showed a refreshing confidence in both her artistic and technical skills.

I caught my breath, and she caught hers, and an awkward silence built between us. She'd reached out, I'd responded, and I didn't know what came next. Maddie set the file on the worktable and hopped up next to it.

I spun on my seat to face her, Maddie's curvaceous fullness right in front of me. I traced her legs muscles with my eyes. "You're strong," I noted.

"I am very strong. And I am very good with tools." She snorted and shook her head. "Sorry. That just slipped out."

"You're incorrigible."

"I know." She leaned back on her hands. Her soft breasts and peaked nipples pushed against her T-shirt.

The woman was a study in contrasts and I wanted to get to know them all. "I know," she repeated. "My corrupted nature has gotten me in my share of trouble. I swore that this year, everything would change."

"And has it?"

She nodded, tears welling her eyes. "It has. And I'm so fucking horny and lonely. Two years, Rhain. *Two years* with no sexual contact, no...touch." Sitting up, she took both my wrists, pressed my hands to her breasts, and just as quickly let me go. "I'm sorry," she whispered. "I shouldn't have done that."

"Why the dry-spell?" I asked, crossing my arms.

"It's in my contract. In red. And all-caps." Before I could ask what she was talking about, her story spilled out, starting with her upbringing in rural New Hampshire, the tally she kept of everyone she'd ever made out with then, then fucked. She made big leaps in time, from her year on a farm, to her year in Scotland with a goddess named Habonde, to meeting Medusa, and back to summers by a lake and something about fireflies above the Winslow's roof.

I tried to absorb everything she said, and knew that if I hung around long enough, I'd hear every chapter of the Maddie Meadows Story.

"But this is terrific," I finally said, when it sounded like she'd spewed all she was going to, tonight. "You have just twenty-three days to go, to fulfill your contract. That's three weeks and change. You've got this, Maddie."

She leaned forward. "Kiss me, Rhain."

"Will that get you in trouble?"

"Oh, I hope so."

Her scent, her yearning, nearly knocked me off the stool. I pressed my hands between my knees and put a few more inches between us. "Then no, I won't kiss you, Madeline Meadows, not yet."

Her cheeks dimpled as she smiled. "Jerk."

"Tease."

"Let me see your tongue." She focused her gaze on my lips. "Give a girl something to look forward to."

"Let me see yours first."

She smiled and licked the corner of her mouth, hid her tongue, licked the other corner, then wet her lips, top and bottom. I groaned hungrily and I might have mumbled something along the lines of, "It's so pink."

Eloquent and profound, how like me. Maddie giggled. I was starting to live for Maddie's giggles. "Pink is my signature color," she said, affecting a Southern drawl. "My tongue is pink, my lips are pinkish-brown, and my other lips are" —she paused and tapped her chin— "Hmm, last time I looked at my pussy in a mirror, those lips ranged from deep rose to a very pale pink."

My knuckles bit into the worktable's wooden surface. "You're killing me, Meadows."

"Oh, it's mutual, Beauchêne. Now stop staring and show me yours."

Following her example, I smiled, then went with my own script. Parting my lips, I curled back the tip of my tongue against the roof of my mouth and undulated the ridged underside. Slowly. Maddie raised one tattooed eyebrow. I took my time unfurling my tongue, extending it in her direction like I was preparing to lick a drip of ice cream off her chin.

I got side-tracked, imagining licking dessert off Maddie's body, and then I offered her the *piece de resistance*. I split the tip of my tongue—one of the few blessings of being stuck in this gargoyle form meant I got to keep the horns *and* the forked tongue—and watched delightedly as Maddie lost her shit.

"Oh, fuck me," she whispered. "Fuck me, fuck me, fuck me."

I stopped showing off. "You can fuck yourself later. I know you know how."

She tucked her hands under her butt. "Let me see that again."

"See what?" Oh, three weeks of foreplay with Maddie Meadows was going to be so much fun.

"Fuck you, Rhain. Let me see your tongue."

I did.

"Can you move just the tips?"

"I can." I stayed still. I wanted her to ask for it.

"Rhain, would you *please* show me what you can do with your forked tongue?"

I split the tip as far as I could and showed her how I could keep a wide V as I licked up and down, down and up. I showed her how I could shimmy the tips and create a vibration. Maddie liked that. A rosy blush blanketed her cheeks and she whimpered.

Gods, she looked adorable. Adorable, delectable, and fuckable.

"More," she grunted.

"Nope." Never had one word cost me so much. "I want to get back to what you said about the usual orifices. You said you had idea and then you waved this around." I palmed the "S" file and showed it to her.

"Uff, that was *before* you used your tongue to distract me."

"I showed you because you asked nicely."

She stuck out the tip of her tongue and wagged it at me.

"Brat."

"I've been called worse." She eyed the file, then my crotch, and sighed. "Is there anything you could take that would knock you out long enough for me to work on your...obelisk?"

"You saying you want to polish my knob?"

Maddie pressed her hand to my mouth. "Goddess and Spirit, would you stop? Answer my question."

I tickled her knuckles with the tips of my split tongue. She jerked her hand away and swiped it on her shirt.

"How fast can you work?" I asked.

"Give me an hour the first time, and I'll be able to judge from there."

"An *hour*?" It was my turn to groan in frustration. "Maddie, I can make myself come. I'll fall apart, which'll give you five minutes, ten tops, to work on me. Then you'll have to speak the spell that makes me whole or I'm—"

"Toast?"

"I was going to say gravel for the fish tank."

"I suck at metaphors."

"I could ask my brother to wait outside the room and have him speak the spell. Would that take some of the pressure off?" At her vigorous nod, I added, "Then I'll do it. I'll let you work on me."

She squealed, threw her arms around my neck, and froze. Barely breathing, I waited for her joyful squeal to turn into a scream of pain and when it didn't, I noticed Maddie relaxing into the embrace, breath by breath, ounce by ounce. I stayed still.

Goddess knew, I was good at staying still.

"Hug me," she pleaded. "Please."

Ever so gently, I wrapped my arms around the half-fae chiseling her way through the cracks in my carapace and inhaled the faint scent of her soap.

She'd found my horns and was distractedly stroking them from base to tip. I was getting harder. And Maddie's body was getting heavier. She untangled her arm and traced my length through my pants. Gently, I took her by the wrist and moved her hand away.

"Day after tomorrow, my brother Trey can take Daffyd's shift, and we'll get started."

Chapter Eight
MADDIE MEADOWS

Meeting Rhain in person wrecked me in the best way. He was everything I'd been fantasizing about and more, *so* much more. I almost felt guilty about begging him to kiss me, and I really, *really* admired his self-control.

He left the same way he arrived. After locking the window, I returned to my studio to muse on the technical process of taking his cock from an unfinished obelisk to something I wanted in my vagina. Which led me to think I should research the history of dildos. I opened my laptop and wandered through images until the need to pee and brush my teeth finally forced me to get up. I wandered through every room of my condo, brushing way past the usual three minutes while wondering how it would feel to share this space with a gargoyle.

"That is way too much, way too fast, even for *you*, Maddie Meadows," I chided my reflection in the mirror over the sink. "He's coming over because you have the tools and expertise to fix his problem. Use the opportunity to get to know him and *then* you can figure out how to safely jump his bones."

This year as Medusa's proxy was my chance to reform every damn reckless habit that had fucked me over in the past. Rushing headlong into inserting my latest lover into my life, or inserting myself into theirs, was one of my top three worst traits. It never worked out and most times, I'd known within *hours* I'd made a mistake. Besides, my final project for the sculpture class was due the first week of May and that had to be my primary focus. Though if Rhain was serious about letting me use my tools on him—

Foamy toothpaste overflowed the corner of my mouth. Blessed Hedone, I might have figured out a final project that would both showcase my skill and give us what we each wanted.

I rinsed off the mess I'd made, slipped my feet into house slippers, and headed right back to my studio. I could jot down my idea in one of my sketchbooks, maybe start building an armature...

I ENDED up working on my idea until two in the morning. Medusa's ringtone woke me, trilling from the kitchen counter at the un-goddess-like hour of seven-thirty. I stumbled out of bed and jabbed at the speaker phone icon.

"Hey." My voice was nearly as gravelly as Rhain's and sounded way less sexy to my ears.

"'Hay'? Hay is for horses, Madeline. I believe the proper greeting would be more along the lines of, 'Good day, my Lady.' And then I would hear your knees hitting the floor."

I filled my new electric water kettle, set it on its stand, grabbed my phone, and headed down the hall. "And then you'd hear me scream because I'm almost to the bathroom and the floor in there is tile."

Medusa laughed. "Oh, Madeline, I shall miss our chats."

Tucking the fluffy bathmat under my shins, I sank onto the backs of my heels, confessing, "I'll miss them too, my Lady."

"Oh, stop. You don't really have to call me that."

"I know." I fumbled for the first hat box's lid and lifted it slowly. Startling a viper was never a good idea. "But you're a goddess in my eyes and it is my pleasure to serve you."

"How are my darlings?"

"They're well."

"And you're all still getting along?"

I giggled. "I think we all might be a little sex-starved."

Medusa roared with laughter. "I can empathize. I seem to have made up for my lengthy dry spell. Which leads to the reason for my call. What would you say to being my proxy one month of every year? And maybe the occasional long weekend? And a holiday or two? We could even, oh, I don't know, vacation together."

I'd had a feeling Medusa would ask me this, and I'd already considered my answer. "I would be honored. I think the girls like me, and I found a great vet who—"

"A great what?"

"Vet. Short for veterinarian. A doctor who works with

animals. And reptiles. I scheduled all the girls for their annual check-ups. Doctor Wanamaker comes highly recommended."

"You're taking my snakes to a *doctor*? Why in the Gorgon's name would you do that?"

"Because you charged me with keeping them healthy? Because I recently moved to Manhattan, and I'm worried they're stressed?"

"Stressed because you changed which state you lived?" She must have pulled her phone away from her face for another good laugh. "Oh, my dear girl, I shouldn't make fun. Your attention to my magnificent seven simply reinforces I chose well when I chose you."

I didn't remind her there was no one else in line for the job. And that Habonde was instrumental in preparing me to serve *my Lady*. "Thank you. Was there anything else you wanted?"

"One thing. I purchased the penthouse above your new home. Actually, I purchased the entire building. Georges and Désirée have agreed to stay on in their current positions."

It was a good thing I was sitting. "You bought the *Belleport*?"

"Yes. I like the neighborhood. I like the fact there's a mansion full of dragons and Magicals across the street. And I need a home base. New York's possibilities are endless, and these eleven months have opened my eyes, Madeline. I have wallowed in self-pity far too long."

How should I respond?

"It's a nice building. I think you'll like it here. The neighbors are nice too."

"Are you speaking of a particular neighbor? One Rhain Beauchêne, perhaps?" she asked, saying his name in proper Welsh, which only worsened my obsession.

"He's one of the gargoyles who watches from the dragons' roof. How did you know he was the neighbor I was talking about?"

"Habonde mentioned him. Introduce us when I arrive on the twenty-eighth. Ta until then."

"Ta."

I remained in a state of semi-shock after Medusa ended the call. Would having her living above me be like living with my mother? I shuddered at the thought. Medusa's maternal feelings were reserved for her snakes, and though I could see us becoming friends—

One thing at a time, Maddie. One thing at a time. Transfer the girls to their snake tower, cue up their favorite easy-listening jazz channel, put on your pants, and get to class.

ANOTHER SHOCK WAITED for me at the Academy of Art. Once everyone had straggled in, settling noisily at their separate worktables and cracking the lids of their to-go cups, Professor Hepplewhite cleared his throat.

"You are aware your pieces for the upcoming finals are due May first." He waved away the few groans. "This gives Academy faculty three days to review your work before the exhibit."

Most of us nodded. He repeated due dates and expectations at every class. The perpetually late succubus closed her eyes and banged her forehead on her table.

"I was given a piece of exciting news over the weekend." Professor Hepplewhite clasped his hands to his chest and took a deep breath. "This class has been invited to hold their final exhibit at the Winslow Gallery of Art. I ran into their gallerist, who was a student of mine, and Helia extended the invitation.

"The *Winslow*," he exhaled, sending his gaze heavenward.

"And this is a good thing?" someone had the audacity to ask. Basking in the fluorescent light, Professor Hepplewhite ignored the question.

"Opening night will be black tie formal. You *will* bathe and you *will* dress appropriately. Helia confided that Mr. And Mrs. Winslow *themselves* will likely host the reception."

Professor Hepplewhite almost swooned at his own words before pulling himself together. "Your pieces will be moved to the gallery on the fourth, cleaned and placed, and doors open at six on Friday evening. Any questions?" He scanned the room, ignoring the rumble of sleepy minds coming to grips with the gift we'd been offered. "No? Good. Get to work. Madeline, I need to speak with you."

I *knew* that was coming. I met him in the corner, at his desk.

"Where is your piece?" Before yesterday, I didn't have a piece or even an inspiration for a piece, which I thought I'd very skillfully kept secret by constantly sketching, or modelling clay, and looking deeply preoccupied during class.

"I'm working on it at home and it's too big to carry back and forth."

"Will you have any trouble getting your piece here, or do you expect the faculty to come to you?" Professor Hepplewhite's tone was growing increasingly condescending.

"I—" Oof, I hadn't thought that part of through. I was saved by the lightbulb that occasionally flashed its brilliance in my head. "I live near the Winslows." Words tumbled out of my mouth before I had time to regret my idea. "My studio's in my building. I would be happy to have you and your colleagues over, and then I can arrange to just have my piece moved across the street.

"It's big," I added, scrambling to make up a plausible story, "and heavy, but I know some people who can help me move it and—"

"Ms. Meadows, if you can afford to live *across the street* from the Winslows, you can afford to feed us if we're trekking all the way to the Upper East Side. I'll expect a catered breakfast and booze. You have the" —he consulted his coffee ring-stained paper calendar— "first slot Monday morning, nine o'clock sharp."

"Thank you." Relieved, I turned to go.

"A pitcher of Bellini's would suffice. And I'm allergic to gluten," he added, speaking to my back. I waggled my fingers over my shoulder. *Okie dokie then.* I slipped my winter coat back on and grabbed my courier bag. Time to visit Rhain and give him the news.

A HANDSOMELY UNIFORMED man greeted me in the Winslow's lobby. I introduced myself as Madeline, not Maddie, and searched his jacket for a name tag.

"Is Rhain expecting you?" Aravind asked.

"Yes and no. He's posing for me—I'm a sculptress—and I need to talk to him about scheduling our next session."

He blanched. "A sculptress?"

"I...I sculpt, yes."

He peered at me more closely. "You're fae."

"Half-fae, half-human," I corrected. "I can hold a decent glamour and I can see other Magicals who're using fae glamours. I can even see the wards protecting this building and the rooftop area. I live in the Belleport."

Aravind nodded as if that explained everything. I started to say more as the *whoosh* of an inner door opening and the steady tap of stiletto heels announced another visitor.

"Aravind, why don't you leave Mr. Beauchêne's visitor with me while you make the necessary arrangements to see her to the roof?"

I remembered to close my gaping mouth before I turned to see who'd spoken.

"Hello. I'm Helia." A striking individual paused and extended their arm. "I run the gallery and I believe you're one of Professor Hepplewhite's students? Either that or there are two sculptresses named Madeline Meadows working in New York City."

Helia's smile was warm and inviting, their makeup flawless, and I didn't even want to guess at the retail price of their exquisitely tailored suit. I shook their hand and grinned. "Yes, I'm one of his students. He told us this morning we're going to have our senior show here, in your gallery, and I'm—" I flapped my arms.

"A bird?" Helia laughed gently and gestured toward the

set of glass doors leading away from the lobby. "Come have a look at the space while you wait for Aravind to return." She opened one of the doors and waited for me to enter. "Watch your step. We're having a new floor put in."

Light filled the cavernous room. Double height ceilings soared overhead, while un-curtained windows faced Park Avenue.

"This is gorgeous!" I gasped, picturing myself in a gown, on one of the tufted velvet window seats, sipping champagne and dazzling patrons with my witty conversation. Helia's voice interrupted my fantasy.

"We have a lot to do before May fifth. I'm taking it as a sign from Goddess and Spirit that I ran into Professor Hepplewhite. Re-opening Winslow Fine Art Gallery with a show of student work speaks to the hope we place in the coming generations of artists."

"That's a lovely sentiment," I said.

"Mr. Beauchêne is waiting for you." Aravind waved from the door. "Helia, could you keep your ears open for visitors? I've locked the front door. If someone rings and you don't feel comfortable letting them in, I've also left a note saying I'll be back in a flash."

"Thank you, darling. I appreciate you looking out for me."

There was a story behind his gesture and the flash of marble white as Helia's cheeks lost their color. I followed Aravind to the private elevator, refrained from gawking at the opulence as we stepped into the foyer on the fourth floor, and breathed more freely once he unlocked and opened the door to the rooftop area.

"Do you need me to fetch you when you're finished?" he asked.

"I can find my way down."

"I left the gate to the fire escape unlocked." He pointed to the far corner. Beyond, I noticed the Belleport. "That gives you access to the gargoyles."

Chapter Nine

RHAIN BEAUCHÊNE

I felt Maddie approach. She stopped behind me and nudged my back with her knees. Checking my glamour and finding it weakened, I refreshed the spell and shot her a grin as I stood.

"I talked to my brother. He's on board with our idea."

"That's great, Rhain." She wrapped her arms around my chest. Her heavy wool coat was a good choice. "And I've had another idea," she added, letting me go. "And Medusa called. But let me tell you my idea first. Oh, and there's been a development with my sculpture class and the group show."

"I'm all ears."

"It's not your ears I want, it's your horns." Batting her lashes, she lifted her bag's strap over her head and looked for a place to set it down. The rooftop was covered in slushy rain from the morning's sleet-fest. I took the bag from her.

"They don't come off, you know."

"Very funny." She crossed her arms and stared at the

top of my head. "Seriously, I want to start with your horns. Whatever material your stone is—"

"It's marble," I interjected, "but let's talk someplace where I'm not terrified you'll slip or fall." The narrow walkway connecting the four corners wasn't a great place to have a conversation with someone as animated as Maddie. Taking hold of her elbow, I guided her through the gate and onto the roof. "Saint Laurent marble. Clan Beauchêne is from France."

She nodded knowingly. "Let me get familiar with your stone skin by starting with your horns. I looked it up, and your horns don't have nerve endings, except at the root. Right now, their surface is pitted and dull, likely from all the hours you spend out here in all kinds of weather. If you let me smooth and polish the marble while you're awake, it'll get you used to the touch of my tools. Plus, it'll let me get to know you, know what you're made of, so when I go to work on the obelisk, we'll both be better prepared."

I reached up and felt along the length of one of my horns. Maddie was right, the surface had gotten rougher. With a love interest in my life, I sensed my grooming habits were about to get an upgrade.

"You saying you want me smooth and shiny?"

She nibbled at her lower lip and blushed. "I do. I have all kinds of plans for you, baby. Stick with me, you'll be ready for showtime in no time."

I laughed along, then asked about her conversation with Medusa. She laid it all out and finished up with, "I said yes."

"I'm happy for you. Happy for me too. Now what's the news with your show?"

Maddie bounced on her toes and spun in place, sending a spray of slush against my shins. "My professor arranged for us to have it here, at the Winslow's *gallery*."

"That's great!"

"There's more." She took in a deep breath and tucked prayerful hands under her chin. "I want you to be my final project."

Dread weighted my legs in place. "I don't understand."

"You're capable of sitting still for hours. All I would need is for you to stay still for a few hours at a time, say during my review, when all the professors in the art department will come to my studio to evaluate my work, and then during the show. We could tell Helia and Aravind and whoever else needs to know what we're doing."

My discomfort must have showed on my face. Maddie patted my cheeks with mittened hands and barreled ahead. "Rhain, imagine it. You, reclining on a marble base, in your stone skin. And just these two touches of polished perfection, your horns, and your cock. With the right lighting, I can make the marble glow and with these veins" —she trailed her finger along a particularly thick slash of white— "and the coppery ones, it'll be this study in contrasts. 'The Monster and the Man.' It'll be epic. Erotic. And sexy."

The idea of putting myself on display in a room full art critics unleashed a swell of memories. The unpleasant kind, the kind I'd paid a therapist to help me put to rest.

"Rhain?"

I lifted my face to the sky, the way agonized lovers did in movies, and was rewarded with a splat of sleet landing in one eye. I wiped it off and met Maddie's expectant expression.

"I'm on board for what you want to do to my body parts if it's to make physical intimacy possible between us. Possible and pleasurable. But I'm not— I mean, I can't put myself on display like that, Maddie. I've dealt with people's lack of understanding about my situation enough to last a lifetime.

"I can't do this for you. Ask me for something else, anything else. Ask me to pose for you. That, I can and would do."

I hated seeing confusion and frustration flash across Maddie's face, before turning to despair. "I'm out of ideas, Rhain, and I'm terrified I won't bring this project to the finish line. Which is the story of my life: Maddie Meadows, the girl who jumped in too fast, quit too early, and never, ever, lived up to anyone's expectations."

"Maybe you'll get inspired while you're working on my—" I looked down. Maddie looked down. My dick knew it was the topic of conversation, so it twitched. "See? He agrees."

She snorted softly and tugged on the strap clenched in my hand. "I'll figure something out."

"I have faith in you," I said, releasing her bag. "When's our first session?"

"I'll have my people get in touch with your people."

"You could post a note on your window."

Deeply conflicted about our differing visions, I watched Maddie traverse the rooftop and disappear behind the door to the stairwell. She didn't look back. I waited to see her cross the street to her building before I descended the fire escape and entered the Winslow's lobby. Aravind had been joined by his cousin, Kunal.

"Guys, do either of you know if the Belleport has underground storage for their tenants?"

"Yeah, they do," Kunal said. "Not sure how up to date it is."

"Great. There's something I'd like your help with." I outlined my plan, then asked if they or possibly the Winslows knew how I might get in touch with Medusa.

"Medusa, as in the Gorgon?" Aravind asked. "She was beheaded, wasn't she?"

"She was, but you know how those myths go. Most of the time, what gets retold and written down is the showy stuff. Apparently, she was reunited with her head and now Maddie's working for her."

"Why can't you just ask her?"

"Because then she'll know I'm planning a surprise."

I RETURNED to my rooftop post with something like a skip to my step. While in the lobby, I'd also placed a call to my mother, Rhoswen, head of Clan Beauchêne, setting an important piece of my plan into motion. I swung by Daffyd's corner and let him know our first session with Maddie was happening at her place the next night.

"The things I do for you."

"I'm grateful, bro."

"And I'm glad I can help." He stayed in his crouch, his

empty eyes gazing beyond Central Park. "So, Maddie is Medusa's proxy. I ever tell you I had a crush on Medusa?"

I sat on the balustrade, my back to the Park. "*Had?*"

His laugh rumbled deep in his pitted marble chest. "Have. I always thought a gargoyle would be a logical choice for her to take as a lover."

"If Maddie's idea works, I hope I can talk her into wearing the snakes when we, y'know—"

"Kinky."

"Oh, you have no idea the scenes I've imagined."

"Bet I do."

We stopped talking and I was pretty sure Dai's mind had taken him the same place as mine, only with a different partner.

"I want to meet Medusa," he finally said, breaking the silence. "If she's ever in town."

Chapter Ten

MADDIE MEADOWS

Suddenly, I felt like my life was going off the rails. I'd moved into my condo ten days ago and in those ten days, I'd met a guy and maybe lost a guy.

Wasn't my shortest relationship on record.

And maybe I hadn't lost Rhain. I'd upset him because I let my mouth run off with an idea before giving my head enough time to consider the pros and cons. Good news was, Rhain wanted to go ahead with "Project: Refine My Appendage," which was beginning to sound more and more like some kind of elective surgery or cosmetic procedure.

At least that made me laugh and if he could get over this bump in the road, I could too. Now that we'd talked things out, I could cool my horny heels, finish my contract with Medusa, and put my attention where it should be, on my art. I planned to take all of March and April to execute and finish my final project.

All I needed was a different idea.

Correction, all I needed was a *better* idea, one my

newest friend and future lover didn't find inherently insulting. I shrugged off the waves of shame that used to send me into my shortest, tightest dress and the nearest pick-up bar and picked up my sketch pad. I had a final project to design and zero time to waste.

"MS. MEADOWS, please see me in my office." Professor Hepplewhite, who was standing right behind me, projected his voice so the entire class could hear. The girl working beside me snickered. I willed her wire armature to collapse under the weight of her reductive interpretation of the human body.

Fortunately for her, it didn't.

"Coming, Professor."

Three weeks after I'd insulted Rhain, I continued to struggle every time I showed up to class. I threw a damp towel over the block of uninspired clay I'd tried to make "Come alive!" as Professor Hepplewhite admonished over and over. The grayish lump looked every bit as lifeless and inert as it had when I first slapped it on the plastic-covered table.

"I'm having doubts about your ability to successfully complete your final project in time. Convince me I'm wrong."

He took a seat behind the desk in the corner of the room farthest from the door. From here, he could see every student and every project, and everyone was farther into their piece than me.

"I'm still looking for the right model." I feigned exasperation with my predicament.

"What of the models in your life drawing class?"

I shook my head. "No."

"Look again. What material are you planning to use?"

I glanced over my shoulder at the lump of clay. Its sorry shape accused me of neglect. "I don't know."

"Then please tell me what you do know."

Medusa would be in Manhattan in less than twenty-four hours to take possession of her snakes and move into the Belleport. I grabbed onto that fact. "My job contract ends tomorrow. After that, I'm free to focus solely on this project."

"Have your sketches ready for review on Monday. We'll fill out your materials requisition form and submit it." Gripping the edge of his desk, he leaned forward, leering. "If I am not satisfied you can complete this project in time for the opening, you're out, Ms. Meadows. O. U. T. Out. Do you understand?"

Hot tears splashed my cheeks the moment I escaped the classroom. Keeping my head low, I stumbled down the back stairs and exited onto a side street. It took me a moment to get my bearings, and once I did, I lifted my face to the soft rain long enough to cool my cheeks, then called for a Broom car to get me home.

MY FINAL HOURS as Medusa's proxy were blessedly uneventful. Habonde and I met via video and by the time she and I finished our debrief, sun shone through my windows. Medusa joined us for the second hour. I ordered deli sandwiches to be delivered and we feasted on pickles, chips, and Reubens while we chatted. Habonde supported Medusa's idea to have me fill in for her one weekend a month and noted the same kind of arrangement could work to entice other Goddesses and neglected Magicals to participate in her program.

After I showered, Medusa took me shopping for a gown to wear to the opening of the art show. I had to keep steering her away from ones that were Met Gala-ready, to dresses I would get more wear out of.

"Madeline, what is it with you? No one amortizes the cost of a dress. No. One."

"I do," I said, crossing my arms.

"Tell me, have you figured in the 'Wow!' factor? And what's the expression on your boyfriend's face worth, huh? Get the dress that makes you feel like a bloody queen." She skidded to a stop. "Wait. *I'm* buying the dress."

"Yes, and I'm buying the accessories. Do you have any idea how much that's going to add to the price of an evening that'll last all of what, four, five hours?" I shot back.

"Madeline Meadows, you helped me. Granted, I paid you to help me, and you did sign a contract. Now, I'm helping you."

I caved. Medusa chose my dress, and, in the end, I loved it. She put me in charge of booking my own spa treatments with, "Have you seen your skin? It looks like you've been rolling in marble dust!"

After our day was done, and our purchases accounted for and *ooh*'d over, I helped carry her beloved girls to the penthouse. Through multiple elevator trips up one flight, I described each snake's food, light, sleep, and music preferences, and let Medusa know I'd ordered another custom-made tree house just like the one in my condo.

"You're going to miss them, aren't you?" she asked. I nodded, and she dismissed my tears with a *pffft*, adding, "We'll get you your own. I'll give you snakes; you can design me some hats."

"Oh, you can borrow anything in my closet."

She stopped mid-step. "Borrow clothes? Who borrows clothes?"

"Me and my friends used to do it all the time."

"I should tell this to my sisters."

I had no idea Sthenno and Euryale were alive. I kept my surprise and my questions in check. I had work to do, so much work, and none of my ideas were coming together in the way I wanted.

At least I had ideas. "I'm going to go have a bath."

"Goodnight, Madeline. And thank you."

I locked my door and leaned against it, staring into my home. I'd come to love the snakes and the rooms felt empty without them and their hat boxes. I opened the refrigerator and couldn't find anything appetizing. I opened my laptop to look for a movie to stream while I soaked. Nothing suited my mood. I couldn't even put a finger on my mood. Maybe my period was getting close.

My gaze raked the Winslow's rooftop, searching for Rhain. He waved. I waved back, and then I just stood there staring across the abyss separating us until it sunk in: my year of celibacy was up, Medusa had her snakes, and I was free to fuck whomever I wanted. And the only one I wanted was standing in the sleet. I hadn't finished working on his cock, but there were other tools in both our boxes, starting with his tongue.

I ran into the kitchen and rifled through the various envelopes and the messages I'd written on their backs, searching for the one that would bring Rhain here in record time. The best I could do was re-use the first message I'd ever written, "HELP."

He read the note, straightened his legs, and tore off the roof. I made it to the room with the fire escape in time to hear footsteps pounding the metal grates and see his horns, then his face, and the rest of his gorgeousness appear, slick with rain.

"Maddie," he said, breathing hard, "I have something for you. I was waiting for Medusa to leave."

"I have something for you too." I cocked my hip to the side and rolled my shoulder.

"Can yours wait?" he asked, hesitating.

"Uh, sure."

"Meet me in the lobby. I don't want to track slush through your rooms."

This wasn't the romantic reunion my pussy and I were counting on. I accepted the brief delay, grabbed a flannel shirt and my keys, and hit the elevator button. Rhain was waiting for me, smiling ear to ear.

"C'mon."

He grabbed my hand. Shuffling my feet, I jammed my toes deeper into my slippers. "Where're we going?"

"Downstairs."

"Ooh, a basement rendezvous. How romantic!"

He ignored me, leading me through a door I'd never used

and down a dingy set of stairs I hoped never to use again and into the Belleport's communal storage locker area. A single bare light bulb didn't provide nearly enough light. Against my better judgement, I let Rhain drag me between the rows of fenced cages. We stopped at the big metal door at the end.

"What's this?"

"*This* is my contribution to your final project." He dangled a ring with two heavy keys in my face. I grabbed them both and hovered the tip of one in front of the lock. My hand shook. "I sprayed it with WD40," he added. "Should slide in easily now."

"Getting right to the lubrication part of my surprise, hmm?"

His deep, rumbly laugh weakened my knees. It was a good thing the key slid in, and the lock gave. Rhain cupped one hand over my eyes. I pushed on the door. Bright light bled in and around his fingers. The room smelled like *new*, and I loved new. I couldn't stop myself from bouncing on my toes.

"Rhain, c'mon!"

"Ta-da!"

Blinking, I tried to take in what I was seeing—a fucking sculpting studio with a kiln and enough room to create life-sized pieces—but my brain couldn't process what it all meant. I grabbed Rhain's arm for stability. Patiently, he led me to the first of two heavy worktables. A canvas tarp covered a blocky shape.

"Pull on it, Maddie."

I gathered the corner of the tarp and pulled, revealing a block of rough marble the same color as Rhain.

"Oh, my Goddess."

"There's more," he said. "I had my mother ship the marble from France. I asked Helia for advice on what tools and things you needed. They're the ones who insisted we install a new air filtration system."

"You did this for me."

"You're the artist, Mads."

"But we haven't even—"

"Let me show you everything. Medusa okayed turning this room into your studio. Now that you're not taking care of her snakes, all you have to do is make art."

I left Rhain's side and ran my hands over the hunk of marble. Six feet long and four feet high, the stone pulsed with possibility.

"I can't wait to start," I whispered.

"You can start right now. I'm on duty tonight, so I've got to get back."

I released the block of stone long enough to grab Rhain's face and plant a kiss on his cool lips. "Thank you."

"You're welcome, Madeline."

Rhain left. I hurried back up to the fourth floor to gather a fresh sketchbook, sticks of compressed charcoal, gum erasers, steel-toed boots, everything I'd need—except, I'd forgotten to tell Rhain why I'd called him over in the first place.

For the first time in my life, my libido lost out to an overwhelming desire to draw, to...to create. I filled a water bottle, locked my door, and started the process of exploring Rhain's amazing gift.

F riday night. There was nothing left for me to do except get into my outfit, take the elevator to the Belleport's lobby, and walk to the Winslow mansion. Medusa had checked in on me earlier, on her way to meet Daffyd. He was taking her to dinner at an exclusive Magicals-only restaurant and her way of dealing with a raging case of nerves was to over-mother me. I assured her I was fine, had everything I needed, and shooed her toward the elevator.

Eyes wide with fear, she clamped her gloved hands against the opened doors. "Madeline, I have never in my life been on a formal *date* with a *man*. What do I *do*?"

"You order a drink, you look at the menu, you allow him to compliment you on your dress." I retied the belt on my bathrobe. Reaching into the elevator, I pressed the button to keep the doors from closing and studied the woman in front of me. She'd chosen a strapless satin floor-length gown in midnight blue. Her retinue of snakes had been quieted by the gem-encrusted eye masks

Daffyd commissioned from an alchemist who was also a jeweler. The spells in those accessories would buy Medusa six worry-free hours to drink, dine, dance—and attend the art show—without fear of turning anyone to stone.

Medusa nodded, then stared at me. "What else? I understand finding sexual partners. I don't understand this... this... *romance* stuff."

No wonder she and I had gotten along from the get-go. "Gaze into his eyes and ask him questions. Avoid eating a lot of garlic. He's going to want to kiss you, you know." I checked the clasps on her diamond bracelets and adjusted her cloak's generous hood. I didn't want the girls catching a chill. "Be yourself, Medusa."

"Okay," she whispered. I peeled her fingers off the door, released the stop button, and blew her a kiss.

Showtime.

The dress Medusa and I had chosen together hung in its bag. I'd find another event to wear it, one Rhain and I could attend together, without either of us having to hide behind a glamour. The outfit I planned to wear tonight was spread out on my bed.

The closer I'd come to finishing my final project, the closer I'd come to knowing so much more about myself, about how I wanted my creativity represented on my big night. I ended up circumventing Medusa and asking Habonde for help.

"What do you want this costume to accomplish?" she'd asked.

Explaining my concept sounded a lot like I was trying to stuff everything I'd ever learned about Maddie

Meadows into one single, summary paragraph. I finally stopped and expressed the true purpose of my mission.

"I want Rhain to be able to touch me anywhere he wants when he's with me at the opening."

Habonde connected me with a living descendant of the original Fates. I travelled to the demons' Reformed Realm for fittings, which was a trip and a half, and in the process, I made a new friend. Clementine wouldn't be able to attend the opening. She was pregnant with her second child and her demon husband, Prince Laszlo, refused to let her travel. I gave her what-for, even though she was the one holding a cushion full of sharp pins, for caving into her man's demands.

She laughed in agreement, before speaking lovingly about "Laz" and the myriad compromises they both made to honor the mating bond neither wanted to break.

"You two are fated mates?" I'd heard about the phenomenon; I wasn't sure I'd ever met another Magical who been through that experience.

"We are." She'd straightened her legs at that point in our chat and steered me closer to the corner of her atelier equipped with full-length mirrors. "And who knows, you and Rhain might not be fated in the technical sense, but from what you've said, I think magic definitely had a hand in bringing you two together."

I thought a lot about what Clementine said, during the nights Rhain and Daffyd met me in the Belleport's base-ment. The first handful of sessions had been rough. I understood the process I had to follow, which tools to use at each step, but when it came time to handle the pieces of Rhain's fractured body, I damn near threw up. Daffyd's calm, patient presence got me through those early tries. Rhain's pleasure at seeing his transformation bolstered my confidence.

"It's not like you're trying to change me, Mads," he said at one point.

"But I kind of am," I reminded him. "For very selfish reasons, I *am* trying to change you."

"You're trying to change one, external thing and if this change works, it means I can do something I've been wanting to do since I overheard my older brothers talking about sex." He'd grinned at me and patted his ear buds. "Got my music ready. See you on the other side."

AFTER I FINISHED TRANSFORMING Rhain's obelisk into a thing of…of splendor, he and I had barely seen each other. I grew ever more focused on my project, and the Winslows kept sending him out on solo jobs.

Tonight, everything would come together. I moisturized my entire body and stepped my legs one at a time into the jumpsuit Clementine designed. Reaching the zippers required a lot of twisting and grunting and I was glad I'd drawn the shades on the big window. I didn't want anyone seeing me before I was ready, especially not Rhain.

I wiggled my feet into custom-made boots, also courtesy of the Reformed Realm, and retouched my eyeliner. The wind-up clock in the bathroom said it was time to go.

Crossing the street, I added a swagger to my step and glanced down at my shimmery, rose-gold nails, painted to match the inlaid veins in Rhain's forearms. Aravind waved from the lobby as I approached and gave an appreciative whistle.

"Looking good, Ms. Meadows."

"Thank you, Mr. Yadav."

Humans and Magicals mingled near the gallery's wide-open doors. Moving through the crowd, I recognized the faces of other students from both the drawing and sculpture classes. The usually sleepy succubus, adorned in red silk and a pair of gorgeous men, winked at me. I winked back, then headed deeper into the gallery. There was only one man I wanted to see. Though I knew Rhain would be glamoured to look human, I gasped when I finally found him, attired in a well-cut sapphire blue tux and boxed in between two very human females.

My fingers itched to hold a cat's paw tool and pry the bitches off his sides. Lucky for them, Rhain escaped their evil clutches and made his way over to me.

"Hey," he whispered, bending close and kissing the top of my covered head. "You look fucking stunning."

"You do too. We should date."

"We should." He lifted two champagne flutes off a waiter's tray and handed one to me. "Cheers, Madeline Meadows. You did it." We touched the rims of our glasses and sipped. "Now tell my why everyone's pieces are covered up."

"Because we wanted our work to be a surprise."

The gallery grew more packed. Rhain and I couldn't talk long. Professor Hepplewhite insisted on getting pictures of the students standing together, and by the time that was accomplished, Helia had quieted the room.

"Welcome," they began, "to the Winslow Gallery of Art's first annual Student Show. Thanks go to our benefactors, Audrey and Elijah Winslow for hosting this event" —Helia paused and raised their glass to an elegant couple so brimming with dragon magic I had to lock my knees to keep from collapsing— "and to the students of the Academy of Art for allowing us to showcase their work. Professor Hepplewhite, would you introduce the theme of the show?"

A murmur circled among the attendees, and a spot was cleared for the professor. He seemed overcome with emotion, managing only to raise his glass to the room before falling into his husband's arms. Helia took over and stepped to the closest example of student work.

"Could each of you stand beside your piece?"

I moved closer to the middle of the room. My sculpture had a broad base, which required an even broader display box. Like the others, the box was painted flat white. I gave my glass to Rhain and placed my hands on two of the canvas-covered corners. At Helia's nod, I pulled the twelve-by-ten-foot cloth toward me, revealing one roughly chiseled shoulder and the side of a neck. Hearing gasps throughout the room, I quickly finished, drawing the ends of the fabric together and folding and re-folding the tarp to calm my fluttery belly.

With nothing left to do with my hands, I made myself look at the piece that had consumed me for weeks, and which only my professor and his colleagues, and Helia and their helpers, had seen.

The beating heart hiding within the block of marble had revealed itself to me slowly. Before I could find it, I had to find the shape of the man underneath its cool surface.

I heard Rhain give our glasses to a passing waiter. My gargoyle moved closer, until the weight of his presence demanded I either face him and his reaction, or run out of the room.

From behind, he threaded his fingers through mine, something we'd never attempted but which we could now do. Thanks to Clementine's talents with scissors and needles, my entire body was covered in couture canvas held snug to my curves by ingenious darts and cleverly placed zippers. The only exposed skin on my entire body was my face.

"'Invisible Man.' That's a powerful title, Ms. Meadows." Audrey Winslow gazed at my sculpture. It took me a moment to realize her neck ruffs weren't attached to her gown; they extended from the skin.

"It comes apart." I pointed to the where the torso's heart would be and tried to not hyperventilate at my proximity to a dragoness.

"May I?" she asked caressing the figure's chest with fingers tipped in pointy nails and blood red polish. At my nod, she lifted the section of stone. Behind me, Rhain gasped and squeezed my fingers.

With a great deal of time and patience I'd exposed the intertwined veins of white and coppery gold I sensed waiting for me within the very first piece of Saint Laurent marble I'd ever touched—aside from Rhain. I placed my hand over the pectoral area I'd smoothed and smoothed until I swore I could feel a regular pulse travelling through the network of quartz and copper ore.

When I took my hand away, the metallic vein glittered. "This version is called 'Visible Man.'"

"It's amazing," Rhain said, under his breath.

"It's the most exquisite piece in here." Mrs. Winslow waved to Helia. They cut through the crowd, greeted me, introduced themselves to Rhain, and turned to the dragoness.

"I take it you've seen Madeline's work?"

"I have *seen* her work, I have *touched* her work, and now I need one of those little red dots that lets everyone know her work has been sold."

I locked my knees to keep from falling against the gargoyle behind me. "You want to buy *my* piece?"

"Is this not for sale?" Mrs. Winslow shifted her gaze from me, to Rhain, to the sculpture, and back to Rhain. "This is you."

"It is ma'am. And though I know Madeline appreciates your offer, this piece will stay in the Beauchêne family's collection. I must insist."

The dragoness smiled as she nodded. "Then I would commission another, Ms. Meadows. I don't need to see its progress, though I might enjoy watching you work."

"My studio's across the street, at the Belleport. And I would love to have you visit. In fact, I know just the piece of marble for you."

She and Helia got pulled away by other students and parents. I found it impossible to move my legs. "There's no way 'Invisible Man' is leaving my sight," Rhain said.

"There's no one else who should have it."

"Mm," he purred. "Which reminds me, I'm ready to have you."

Chapter Twelve

RHAIN & MADDIE

Maddie faced the big window in her bedroom, where she'd hung strings of bulbs from the center of the ceiling, to the walls. Hundreds of tiny lights glittering overhead gave me the feeling I was outside on a warm, summer night, watching the annual Perseid meteor shower from my rooftop perch. The anticipation of undressing her among the artificial lights was every bit as magical.

She tucked her chin. I pinched the industrial zipper's copper pull between my fingers and let out my breath. Setting my other hand on her shoulder, I started her unveiling, exposing her smooth head and the back of her neck first. The two halves of her form-fitting cap fell to either side with a soft sigh and I continued my task.

I had to go to one knee once Maddie's spine was fully exposed. "Should I keep going?" I asked, because through the combination of magic and ingenious design, the single zipper branched right above her tailbone, sending one zipper down the back of each leg.

"Yes. Take them down together," she said, shifting her feet apart.

"Your wish is my command." Maddie giggled. Her skin pebbled as it was exposed to the air and my breath. I reached her ankles and separated the last bit of each zipper.

"All done."

Straightening slowly, I took a step back and enjoyed the reveal as she shrugged out of one snug sleeve and the other. Arms free, Maddie pulled her entire outfit forward from the waist and dropped it on the floor, leaving her clad in thick-soled, high-heeled ankle boots—and nothing else.

"Turn around," I whispered, sinking onto her bed. A fitted cover made from yet more canvas protected the sheets. Folding forward, I withdrew a wrapped gift box from underneath the bedframe. I'd tipped the concierge to deliver it during the show and waited to hand it to Maddie until after I'd admired her from top to bottom. My gaze stuttered on her dusky nipples and smooth sex. Willing myself to keep my eyes on her face, I offered the box.

"This is for you."

She lifted it, shook gently, and placed it on my upturned palms. Slowly, teasingly, she tugged at the ends of the dark pink velvet ribbon and undid the knot.

"Do you mind if I just tear into the rest of this?"

"It's your gift, Maddie. Tear away."

Grinning, she ripped through the wrapping, lifted the lid, and parted the tissue paper's folds. Lifting the bundle of waxed canvas and leather straps, she shot me a quizzical look. "What're these?"

"Chaps." Maddie found the waist section and shook out the legs. "I had them custom-made for you."

She arched one single, expressive eyebrow. "You're putting me on a horse?"

"I'm putting you on *me*, Ms. Meadows." Understanding dawned across her face. "Shall we give these a whirl?"

Maddie planted her foot on my thigh. I swore the hood of her clitoris peaked out from between her deep-pink labia. "Help me out of my boots first."

"My pleasure." Another of the oversized copper pulls dangled from the back of the boot. "I appreciate the thought you put into the design of your outfit."

"I was hoping you'd be the one to undress me," she said, slipping her foot out, removing the sock, and lifting her other foot.

"And I was hoping you'd ask." I set both boots on the floor next to the bed and took the chaps. "Let me show you how this works."

I fastened the belt piece around Maddie's waist, wrapped one leg, and drew the zipper up. As soon as I repeated the same thing with the other leg, she grabbed hold of my knees and sank into a wide plie.

I lost my ability to communicate with words, especially once she straightened her legs and came close enough I could smell her arousal. "Grab my horns," I commanded, letting my voice go rough with desire, "and kneel right here." I patted the tops of my thighs.

She held tight. I gripped the backs of her legs and slowly lowered myself onto the bed. Squeezing gently, I lifted Maddie and settled her knees closer to my shoulders. "You're in control."

"Show me your tongue, Rhain."

"Say please."

"Show me your tongue, Rhain. Please." Maddie leaned forward. The weight of her upper body forced my head back. She lifted her hips, dancing above my face. I took my time unfurling my tongue, waiting for her to still her movements, to pout, to ask again before I extended it fully and lapped at her sex.

"Fuck me with your tongue, Rhain. Please."

With the material of her chaps protecting her skin from mine, I urged her knees further apart until she wavered just above my ravenous mouth. Her arms shook.

"Don't let go of the horns," I reminded her. "No matter what." Keeping Maddie safe was every bit as important as fucking her every way we'd planned. I lengthened my tongue again and tasted her for the first time. Musky, tangy, and utterly delicious, I watched her face come undone as I slid my tongue up toward her clitoris, varying the pressure until her body jerked.

I eased off, probed deeper, deeper, until her lips pressed against mine. And then I fucked Maddie Meadows with my tongue, letting the muscle go thick and strong, pulling out enough I could nudge at her clit.

"Stop." I stilled. Maddie's whole body twitched. "I don't want to come yet."

"You want to come on me." She bobbed her head up and down, never opening her eyes. "You're wet enough to take me, Maddie. Let me see your beautiful clit first."

She released my horns one at a time and spread her labia. "She likes pressure," she whispered.

"Show me."

Spreading two fingers, she framed her clit in an upside-down V and eased the pads of her fingers along its sides. I swept the split tip of my tongue between her fingers and the engorged hood, following along with Maddie's stroke. She whimpered.

"I don't wanna hold back."

"You don't have to hold back."

"But I wanna fuck your gorgeous cock."

I let go of her leg and popped the cap on the bottle of lube. "Then fuck me. I'm all yours."

Maddie walked backward on her knees, a drugged look in her eyes. I propped myself on one elbow and spread lubricant all over the newly smooth surface. Pressing my thumb against the base to keep it vertical, I glanced up at Maddie.

"Go slow. This is a first for both of us."

Her gaze rapt, she held my wrist and lowered herself until I couldn't see my cock's rounded head. I needed to mark the moment. I was about to not be a virgin anymore, at least in this aspect of sexual experience, and the sensations were as overwhelming as the odd cracking inside my chest.

"Stop." My voice broke. "I need to savor you."

"I've done this so many times, but *this*—" She shook her head. "This is different."

"Could you look at me?"

I needed to know she wasn't afraid or repulsed. I needed to know she wanted me, Rhain the gargoyle; not

Rhain, the art project or the problem to be solved; not Rhain, the novelty fuck.

I GAZED DOWN AT RHAIN, at him trying so hard to process everything he was feeling. Words gathered in my belly and my chest, turning in on themselves and refusing to leave. My body took over, softening my thigh muscles so I could ease my way down, and up a little, and down, farther this time. Exploring my gargoyle in this way, I fought the need to close my eyes, to lose myself to sensation.

Rhain needed me to watch him. He'd know if I was faking *anything*, so I held his gaze and lost myself in the little flutters and twitches in his eyelids and lashes as his cock stroked my insides.

"Do you need more lube?"

I gently rolled my hips and watched his response. "My body's producing all the wetness it needs. You feel..." I sighed in my search for the perfect word or phrase. "You feel like you were made for me."

"I was, in a way." He raised his softened palms to cup my breasts and I sank forward, delighting in that fit too.

"I wasn't thinking of me as I worked on you," I admitted. "I was following the truth of what was already there."

"Like you did with 'Invisible Man'?"

"Yes."

Rhain stopped talking, following the movement of my hips with his, until my bed was water, and we were waves. I leaned forward more, noticing short, sweet bites of pain where my skin met his, and finally remembered to take hold of the appendages that had caught my imagination the first day we met.

Holding Rhain's horns was the closest I'd come to riding a beast of any kind. He reached behind his head to grab hold of the cover Clementine's demon assistants created for this very purpose.

"Ride me, Madeline."

I did, feeling the smack of my breasts against his chest as I found a way to hold onto my pleasure while avoiding abrasions.

"Where are you?" I asked, noticing drops of my sweat land on Rhain's stone skin.

"I'm right here, ready to go when you are."

"Could you help me? Use your tongue?"

Sweeping his arms down, he cupped my ass, lifted me to his face, and growled. His tongue flicked out, again and again, taking my over-ripe clit to the edge until I begged, "Put me back. Now."

He hovered me over his cock, waiting until he was halfway in before letting go of my ass. Curling his head forward, he flicked my nipples, drawing one into his mouth, then the other, until I screamed for him to stop, to hold still until I could get my bearings.

"Let go, Maddie."

I did, every upward thrust of his pulling guttural sounds from Goddess knew where. He joined in, his voice cracking, propping himself on his elbows, then his hands, changing the angle of his cock until I came again as he exploded inside me. Somehow, I remembered to speak the words that would keep him whole, even while riding him through the aftershocks of his orgasm.

TRYING to find a way to safely lay in each other's arms in the wild, shaky afterglow gave me the giggles. I resorted to covering Rhain's torso and thighs in the biggest towels I had, and leaving his cock exposed for me to fondle and appreciate.

"We did it," he whispered, once I returned to bed with a bottle of champagne. I removed the chaps, put on my bathrobe, and poured generous servings into the tall plastic cups I reserved for iced tea and lemonade.

"I'd like to do it again," I assured him, curling against his side and taking a sip. "And again, and again, and again."

What's Next?

· · ▪ · ◖ · ▪ · ·

More books.

That is literally all I know as I prepare **MEDUSA'S PROXY** for its release. There are many, *many* goddesses and mythological figures clamoring to join the Alliance of the Forgotten and Disremembered; to have proxies trained to take over their roles in the cosmos.

Which leaves me no doubt there is more to come

in 2022.

And 2023.

And beyond.

www.ingramcontent.com/pod-product-compliance
Lightning Source LLC
Chambersburg PA
CBHW020618130626
46552CB00003B/1031